NO
BEAUTIFUL
SHORE

NO BEAUTIFUL SHORE

A NOVEL BY
BEVERLEY STONE

Cormorant Books

Canada Council **Conseil des Arts**
for the Arts **du Canada**

The publisher gratefully acknowledges the support of the
Canada Council for the Arts and the Ontario Arts Council
for its publishing program. We acknowledge the financial support
of the Government of Canada through the Book Publishing
Industry Development Program (BPIDP) for our publishing activities.

Printed and bound in Canada

LIBRARY AND ARCHIVES CANADA CATALOGUING IN PUBLICATION

Stone, Beverley, 1966–
No beautiful shore / Beverley Stone.

ISBN 978-1-897151-19-8

I. Title.

PS8637.T655N6 2008   C813'.6   C2007-906476-0

Cover design: Angel Guerra/Archetype
Text design: Tannice Goddard, Soul Oasis Networking
Cover image: Angel Guerra/Archetype
Printer: Friesens

CORMORANT BOOKS INC.
215 SPADINA AVENUE, STUDIO 230, TORONTO, ON CANADA M5T 2C7
WWW.CORMORANTBOOKS.COM

For Cindy M. Koury,
who taught me how to be a friend

HOW DO YOU LEAVE HOME?

It should be so simple, Bride thought. We are here, and the road leads away from here. She looked out the window and up the road. We could just put one foot in front of the other and follow it, around ponds, over hills, through passageways blasted through the cliffs and off the little island. Then across the causeway and onto the bigger island. And so it would go until eventually we would be somewhere. I believe, thought Bride. I believe in somewhere else.

"The way I see it, we got fuck-all to lose," Wanda said, interrupting the vision of the road that rolled out in front of Bride. Wanda stood with her ass against the countertop, her arms folded across her chest. The little piles of buds lay on the kitchen table between the two girls, broken into lots by eye and hand and without scales. The smell in the air was musky, oily and organic. Wanda sat and took the small, mini-baggies from the box and started to fill them while she talked.

"There's nothing here for us except the same jackasses we went to school with. Now they're bigger. And maybe even dumber." Wanda closed the baggies with her thumb and forefinger, the plastic making a sound like a small insect fluttering its wings. "And no work at all since the fish plant closed."

Bride sat at the table and held her teacup. A large plastic pan of bread dough sat behind Wanda on the countertop, rising in a band of sunlight. "We going to punch down that dough?" she asked, holding the cup to her chest and pointing with her chin.

Wanda looked at the clock. "Few minutes," she said. "I'm almost done." She leaned forward and scraped the remaining weed into a small pile, and then brushed it from the table into her hand. "A bit for later," she said, as if to herself, sniffing it, and then shaking it into a baggie.

Wanda tucked her hands into the pockets of her jeans, pulling them tighter. The waistband was low enough to expose her prominent hip bones, emphasizing the swell of her pelvis against the stick-like boniness of her torso. She wore a grey hooded sweatshirt, unzipped and tucked back behind her arms. Underneath, a lime green tank top drew attention to her complete lack of breasts. Her nipples, visible through the fabric, were larger than a boy's, but otherwise her chest differed little. The bones of her face were hard, giving an angularity to what otherwise would have been a heart-shaped face with apple cheeks and a small chin. She had blue half-moons under her eyes.

Bride went back to the window. The pane of glass took up most of the front side of the little clapboarded house that sat beside the road coming up from the harbour. Vertical wooden racks for drying small, plump capelin lay against the fence. Lynfield had piled a collection of car parts next to the aquamarine K-car that sat up on blocks, the grass growing around it to the window levels. In the front of the house were the other reclaimed things he had dragged up the path: a washer that had rusted from harvest gold to rotten red-brown and a plastic baby bassinet in which Ivey had planted some hopeful flower back in the time when she actually left the house. The bassinet contained a dry twig in hard clay now. A doghouse made of pressboard and green plastic awning sat near the fence, Cereal's unused, oversized chain attached to it.

Wanda continued to talk to Bride's back.

"The way I see it is this — I'll have the money together by the end of the summer. Your grandmother will give you the cash?"

Bride looked down at her sneaker.

"Yeah, she will."

"She was smart to sell your pop's boat when she did. Right before they closed the fishery." Wanda stopped brushing the table. "I got to get that bread punched down. They'll be hungry little fucks tonight."

Upstairs the floor creaked. Bride could see a look of irritation flash in Wanda's face.

"Fuck. Now she's up. Sniffing around for her medicine." Wanda pushed the chair back and the legs scraped the linoleum. She walked over to the stairwell and yelled up.

"Ivey? You stay up there out of my way. I'll bring you the pills."

The footsteps retreated to the back of the house with a slow and heavy tread, a footfall that implied a sigh with each movement.

"That'll shut her up."

"She never says anything, Wanda."

"That's because she's always wacked on these pills." Wanda shook the pill bottle. "You want to stay here?" She pointed toward the empty road, the quiet houses. "Everyone is gone."

∽○∾

A TRUCK STOPPED IN FRONT of the house and a door slammed. Bride turned and watched Lynfield Stuckless walk up the path. He was drunk. He was walking very carefully to avoid staggering, lifting his feet high, keeping his back straight. The small rust-coloured dog flew over the grass to meet him, barking in falsetto, careful to keep a large circle around the man.

"You alright?"

Lynfield staggered two or three steps off the path as he heard her voice.

"Oh my, Wanda. I didn't see you there. I think my eyes are getting worse."

"It's Bride, Mr. Stuckless. Wanda's in the house with the boys."

"Bride. You staying for supper? Wanda got supper on? Good boy, Cereal," he said, not looking toward the dog.

"In the oven. I'm going home though."

Lynfield stood in front of her, wobbling and staring at her with the empty look that blind people have. Bride thought, how is it you can know when someone can't see you? It's not just because they can't focus. It's more like a door into them has been shut.

"If you could just put your arm on mine and take me over to the porch, that would be great."

Bride reached out and led him over to the front of the house. He put his hand on the worn floorboards, stroking the space to make sure that it was clear, and then lowered himself onto it. His knees fell outward and his spine bowed as he let go of the straightness in his back.

"Bride, my eyes is getting worse. That big black spot is getting bigger every day. I can hardly see to get up the path nowadays."

"Hmm."

"You know, I can't see all the bags that people put out sometimes, and Morris has to yell from the cab of the truck to tell me where they are."

Lynfield reached behind him and pulled a flask out of his pocket. He unscrewed the cap and took a drink.

"He's a good head, Morris. Lots of fellows wouldn't have hired me. Morris just laughs about it. He sits there in behind the wheel of the garbage truck and says 'hot' or 'cold' if I miss one."

Lynfield paused a moment and nodded his head. "Eventually I find 'em though. The bags usually stink enough that I don't need to see 'em to find 'em."

"Maybe I should go help Wanda."

"Some good girl, Wanda. What with her mother sick with the nerves and everything."

Wanda's voice came out of the kitchen window, "Sit still you little fucker."

Lynfield shrugged. "Mouth on her though."

"Yes, Mr. Stuckless."

"Some good now that she's finished school that she will be here full time with us. Don't know what we would do without Wanda. Ivey just can't handle it."

Bride smiled and nodded. Then she thought, he can't see that, so then she said, "Yes," and went up the stairs and into the house. Wanda was bandaging Jason's hand in the kitchen.

"... and if he ever says again to hold something while he swings an axe at it, you tell him to fuck right off, you hear?"

Jason nodded in silence, slipped off the chair and went up the stairs.

Wanda turned to look at Bride. "We got to talk about when we go." She took a pack of cigarettes off the counter and lit one. She tilted back her head, exhaled.

"School's over now. We got nothing to keep us here. I need a bit more time to get my shit together, make a bit more money. But I'll be ready by the end of the summer." Wanda paused to inhale. "You got to talk to your mother."

Bride looked away. "Yeah." She paused. "A bit later."

Wanda made a small laughing sound as she exhaled.

"She's going to think I'm running away from her."

"Well, you are," said Wanda.

"Is that what you're doing? Running away from home?"

"Fuck no. All this?" Wanda stretched out her arm.

"I'm sorry, Wanda."

"You got nothing to be sorry for. You're running too. Nobody runs toward anything. They're all just trying to get the fuck away from something."

"Your dad thinks you're going to stay here."

"Surely you're shitting me."

"Nope. Just said how glad he was that you were done school and you're staying home to look after everyone."

Wanda walked away from Bride and looked out the window. "Here? He expects me to stay here?"

"Did you guys talk about it?"

"Me and who? They're both totally checked-out of reality." Wanda knocked on the window with the knuckle of her hand. "Hey," she yelled through the glass. "Keep that little fucker in the yard. Close up the gate so he can't get out in the road."

"You didn't think they'd notice?"

"No. They'll notice. I just thought I'd be gone by the time they did." Wanda started to take the bags of weed off the table and drop them in a khaki green shoulder bag.

"Wanda, who'll look after them when you're gone?"

"They'll be fine."

"They can't be fine on their own."

Wanda paused for a moment and then said, "Fuck, talk about running away. The two of them walked a long time ago." She threw her bag into the corner. "You know what, Bride? I think home ran away from us. Half the people who used to live here are gone now. In fact, I think home ran away from me around the time I was born."

"Okay. Jesus. Stop the drama. I gotta go." Bride pulled her coat on. "Wanda, we forgot the dough."

Wanda stared at her for a moment, and Bride thought, she has the same look as her father, only he really, truly can't see out.

"Fuck. I'm too young to be worrying about bread dough."

∽∘∾

BRIDE STOOD BEHIND THE COMMUNITY centre watching Wanda, whose back was rounded against the clapboard, her head dropped forward. As she raised her hand and smoked, Bride could see that Wanda's nails had been bitten down to the quick. The top shiny layer had been gnawed away so that the ridged undersurface was exposed. The nail beds had hardened into brown, pit-marked pads.

Wanda inhaled with a cocky coolness. She gripped her cigarette almost at the knuckle of her fingers so that they spread across her face at every draw, cupping the projection of her lips. There was masculinity to this embrace of the cigarette. Most girls held smokes at the tips of their fingers, a wand that they waved about as they talked. On the exhale though, Wanda softened back into an eighteen-year-old girl. She sucked the smoke into her mouth and then parted her lips. A cloud of grey rolled out and she inhaled it back through her nose, letting the smoke pour upward like a reverse waterfall. Then she made a pinhole of her lips and pushed the smoke out in a slow, soft stream.

"You got any draws tonight?" said the tall skinny kid standing next to her.

Wanda nodded thoughtfully, looking over his shoulder.

"So how much?"

"Forty, Jackie-boy." Wanda exhaled, her chin tipped upwards, the lower jaw extended.

He dug in his pockets, pulling out a ten from his pants and then a twenty from his jean jacket.

"I got thirty. What will thirty get me?"

"Sweet fuck-all," she said.

"What about I owe you ten?"

"What about you fuck off outta my sight?" Wanda turned away and threw the butt of her cigarette into the bushes.

The boy's face reddened. "I'll pay you. I'm good for it."

Wanda laughed — a hard sound from the back of her throat. She bent over and clutched her stomach, although the sound did not come from there.

"Bitch."

"That's a big word for a little fellow," she said, straightening up.

"From what I hear, you wouldn't know a big fellow from a little

fellow. A carpenter's dream — flat as a board and never been nailed."
The boy's chest filled with air and he held his breath to emphasize
his commitment to the insult.

Wanda had stopped laughing and folded her arms across her
chest. "You know it don't really count as losing your virginity if
your girlfriend goes 'baa' and you come home with wool under your
fingernails."

"Cunt."

Wanda smiled and reached into her pocket for her smokes. "Go
home out of it, before I phones your mother."

He turned and walked away, his back stiff with anger.

"Jaaaack," Wanda called after him. "Come baaack."

"That's a sin for you," said Bride, slapping Wanda on the arm.

"What?" Wanda said. "He didn't have any money," she mum-
bled, the unlit cigarette moving with her lips. She cupped her hand
around the lighter, inhaled and lifted her head.

"No, not the money. The sheep thing."

Wanda shrugged and her lips accompanied her shoulders with a
pout. "He wouldn't have been so worked up about it if it wasn't a
little bit true. If he had never at least thought about it."

Bride smiled. "Let's go in," she said.

"Yeah," Wanda shrugged, "go make some dough, ray, me."

The girls walked around the corner of the community centre. It
had rained earlier in the day and the moisture in the air made the
light full and soft, giving colours density and weight. The evening
blue of the sky was heavy and swollen. A group of cars were parked
around the entranceway. Young men leaned against car doors,
drinking and talking to those seated inside. The sounds of girls'
voices rose over the lower tones of the men, breaking through
their conversations like something small, pointed and sharp. Several
groups turned and watched as Bride and Wanda walked through
the crowd toward the door.

"Hey Bride, you going to give us a little bit tonight?"

Bride did not turn her head to acknowledge Colin as she walked. "Only way you're coming into contact with my bodily fluid is if I spits on ya."

A ripple of laughter spread through the crowd and Colin turned away with a shrug. "I'd do a lot for a night with my head between them big, beautiful titties, I tell you. Even if she can skin you alive with the tongue on her."

"You talking about Wanda?" a voice from inside a car said.

More laughter, this time mostly male, and a voice said, "Wanda. The titless wonder."

Wanda turned toward them. "Fuck off. You'd have to get your heads out of your asses before you put them anywhere else," and continued on toward the community centre, catching up with Bride.

"Yeah, well Bride got enough for both of them," said Colin, raising his hand, stretching out his fingers to make a breast-shaped cup. "Lovely," he said watching her walk up the stairs to the porch.

The laughter was behind them as they stepped into the community centre, lining up to have their hands stamped "paid" in red ink. The music pulsed through the doorway from the stage, pushing outside until the sound waves slowed and died. The beat spread across the harbour, each song throbbing with the same dull rhythm at that distance. They separated, ignoring each other. The DJ was barricaded behind his equipment. As Bride entered the room, she could see only outlines. Then she began to recognize the familiar shapes. Same old crowd, she thought. She looked around the room searching for something different, something that was not the same as every other dance.

Bride walked toward a group of boys, watching the girls in the opposite corner in her peripheral vision, the line of sight reserved for scenery and the apprehension of danger. The boys ignored her approach so she turned in mid-stride toward Wanda, who stood with her back to the wall, close to the fire escape.

"This place is dead. When do you want to get out of here?"

Wanda's eyes moved across the crowd, looking past Bride. "Not yet. I'm just waiting for the boys to come back with some cash. I'll meet you outside."

❦

WANDA STEPPED OUTSIDE AND INHALED the night mist, cold and scented with evergreens. A group of young men stood and watched a couple in a truck under the pole light. The girl's bare leg was draped over the steering wheel. The men stared in silence.

"She's drunk," Wanda said, lighting a cigarette.

"So?" Colin's eyes remained fixed on the couple.

"So tomorrow when you guys tell her what she did, I don't think she's gonna feel very good. She's probably not even feeling that good now."

"Yeah, but Brian is."

"She'd have to be loaded. Brian." Wanda shuddered. "Fuck." She turned and jumped down from the wooden porch of the community centre. None of the boys watched her leave.

Wanda walked down the hill from the dance, the road turning black in front of her as she stepped out of the light. She slowed as her eyes adjusted to the complete darkness, walking at the edge of the pavement, her feet feeling the division between asphalt and gravel. The darkness opened up at the point where the rock face ended and the gravel road to the graveyard began, more grey than black in the spaces between solid objects. She walked more slowly now. She could see darker patches where the road sloped away toward the ditch. The white of the picket fence and the headstones came into view on the left and then the dark shape of Levi's truck. She saw the faint glow of a joint. Levi stood next to his vehicle. She spoke.

"Levi?"

"Wanda. You're late." His voice had a nasal quality, often imitated by others.

"I'm here now. I had a little business to do. You know how it is."

"I'm on time for my business."

She walked close to him now, but could see almost nothing of his face in the dark.

"So let's do some. What'd you want?"

She heard him exhale, and he turned to the truck door, sliding his hand along it to find the handle.

"Get in," he said, the cab light coming on as he opened the door.

Levi was a small man, almost delicate in his bone structure, with a reserve that made others talk more in his presence. His was a considered speech, slow and clear, full of words and sentence constructs that were unfamiliar to outport discourse. Levi often sat in his truck, reading and waiting. In the dark he read by flashlight, parked on wood roads, cemetery lanes and behind closed-up churches. Tonight, a copy of John Stuart Mill's *The Subjection of Women* was wedged into the driver's side dashboard. Alongside it were packages of tissues. He kept the Windex that he used to wipe down the passenger's side of the bench seat in the glovebox.

"Wanda. We have an opportunity here that I need you to consider."

Wanda settled back into the seat. "What?"

Levi did not turn to face her. "There is a growing market here for a lot more than weed. It's cheaper and easier to conceal and very, very lucrative." He put his hands on the steering wheel.

Wanda was quiet for a moment. "You want me to sell pills?"

"There is money to be made."

"What exactly are we talking about?"

Levi continued to stare into the darkness in front of him. "Percocet. You know, the standard prescriptions. A few over-the-counters like E, Special K."

"I'm not selling that shit."

Levi sighed. "Wanda, you're a dealer. What does it matter what kind of drugs you sell? It's like the liquor store refusing to sell tequila."

Wanda slid forward and looked down at the floor. "That shit really fucks people. I don't want no part of that."

"No rock, okay?"

"No, not okay. I don't sell pills."

Levi turned his head now. "Do you hold yourself out as some kind of organic dealer, Wanda? Only Canadian-grown, all-natural produce?" Levi put his head back and started to laugh.

"Look Levi, I'll move the weed for you. But no pills. Too much can happen to your brain on pills."

"An organic vendor with a social conscience. Not the quintessential bay girl."

Wanda cleared her throat. "I think your quintessential bay girl is up the road on her back. You know that's not what I am. I don't sell pills. I'll help you find someone if you want, Levi, but I'm not your girl." She cleared her throat again. "We good here?"

Levi sat still and looked out ahead. "Let me think on this." He paused. "A bit exposed."

"Pick someone you can trust. Like me."

Levi turned to look at her again. "Wanda, I trust you to sell my wares."

"Levi, I don't deal pills. You don't need to take this apart. There's nothing complicated here."

"I think any time a creature acts against its own self-interest there is something very complicated going on, Wanda. Very complicated indeed. That creature usually feels guilt or pride or some other noble sentiment. Or it is in love. Not in love are you, Wanda?"

Wanda laughed. "Levi, you gotta want something from someone to be in love. I've always been good on my own. Like yourself."

Levi shook his head. "Not in love. Some would think that was a sad thing for an eighteen-year-old girl to say. But not me, Wanda, I applaud you. You go away now and think about how many Perks you could move here, and we'll talk again. When you're ready to set aside whatever it is that's making you complicated."

Wanda reached for the door handle. "Yeah, sure. We'll talk. But talk don't change my mind."

"What changes the mind of a woman like you?"

Wanda smiled. "You know that old saying, 'not for love nor money?'"

Levi smiled back. "And we have already established that you're not in love." He laughed now in earnest. "Wanda, I believe I underestimated you."

"That's not such a bad thing, Levi."

"Not for you, perhaps. Not for you." He looked pensive.

"Right, well, not enough high baymen in this cove tonight. Work to do, Levi." Wanda opened the door and jumped out, carefully avoiding the ditch.

"You mind your step there, Wanda."

That was a threat, she thought. "I'm fine. Solid ground here." She slammed the door, and in the open stillness of the cemetery clearing it made a metallic, hollow echo.

"See ya now, Levi."

"We'll talk."

"Yup."

Wanda walked away, her hands in her pockets. Solid ground, with a few big rocks in the path, she thought.

∽∘∾

AS SHE PUSHED THROUGH THE clots of people gathered around the dance floor, talking and being pulled into the moving crowd, Bride watched Wanda work, silent as if she was not in the room but perhaps above it — an eagle watching for movement in water from the face of a cliff. Just before midnight, Wanda disappeared. She was gone for too long to just be having a smoke. Bride glanced back to the corner, but Wanda had not returned. As the lights came up, Bride went outside. The night was misty. The glare of a single pole light made the wet air seem almost steamy despite the spring cold. Cars were slick with the moisture in the air. Windows were sprinkled with pinpricks of water that had beaded there. Bride breathed in and looked around.

Wanda's torso popped out of a car window, passenger side. Her straight blond hair was stringy with the dampness.

"Bride. Over here."

Bride could hear that she was stoned in the slow, even cadence of her summons. Wanda's usual speech was quick and abrupt. Bride walked to where Wanda sat in the window of the car.

"Get in," she said, turning away and using the doorframe to swing her bum inside. Bride could see the shape of a man behind the steering wheel. She opened the back door and sat inside. The smell of Wanda's good weed, her private stock, was strong and earthy. Wanda hung over the front seat. The man turned and smiled.

"My cousin, Wayne," Wanda said. "Home from Fort McMurray."

꘍

WAYNE HAD BEEN LOOKING AT the door of the community centre, listening to Wanda talk, scanning faces for someone he might know. They had all been children when he left. Then Bride stepped out, hesitating on the porch before coming down the stairs, obviously looking for someone. He held his breath and let it out slowly, and thought, I'm stoned, but I can't be that stoned. She was tall for a girl, with long heavy bones that she moved with ease, and looseness in the joints that suggested comfort with herself. Her hair was black and whip straight, cut blunt at the shoulder with a softer fringe over her eyes. As she approached the car, Wayne thought about the incongruity that he saw in her, not quite understanding it at first, not being able to articulate the disconnect. Then he realized that she was female in shape but almost masculine in the way she moved. Her jaw was set hard. She tilted it, listening to someone speak as she walked, smiling. Her shoulders were broader than her bottom. Her arms swung wide, hands open, ready. The heaviness in her shoulders and rib cage enhanced her obvious breasts, and she did not fold forward to hide them as large-breasted women often do. Her shoulders were squared, spine straight. Unlike other girls, she did not walk with little steps designed to swing the ass. Her stride was long and her heels hit the ground hard.

Wayne thought, my fuck. His tongue was dry from the weed and it seemed glued to the roof of his mouth. He swallowed. "What's her name again?"

"Bride."

He handed the joint back to Wanda. "I don't need no more of that."

⌇

IT'S LIKE BEING ABLE TO look at yourself again, eighteen years later. As Bride walked down the path to the roadway, Janice could see herself in a mirror, retreating into the distance. She's my height. She has my body. She even walks with the same step. The maternal resemblance seemed to have skipped a generation in her mother. Myra would say to her, "My glory, Janice, you're just the growth of my poor mother. You're tall like her. You have her long fingers." Gramma Waton's wedding photo hung in the living room, her face sweet and mild against the mug of the man she had married. Grampa Waton was stern, black browed and short. He had married a fair woman with light brown hair, swept back from her wide-eyed face. Bride and I have Grampa's black hair, but our faces are Gramma's, Janice thought. Myra was Grampa's self — 'spit out of him' as she said.

It's hard not to think that I own her, thought Janice. I gave her the skin and bones she walks in. But then again, I live in my Gramma Waton's frame. We are all pieces of someone else. Bride has her father's eyes, set in a Waton's face. God knows whose soul she got. Maybe that is the one thing that does not get handed down.

Janice did not allow herself to think about Brendan much anymore. He had been dead almost as many years as he had been alive.

He did not die all at once for her, but each year Janice felt another small piece of him pass. She did not go to the grave marker anymore. When Bride was little, they went together, bundled up in snowsuits, on the anniversary of the sinking, dragging themselves through the unplowed snow. Janice would always say a prayer that he died fast — "Please Jesus, don't have kept him alive out there in the water and the dark, half-froze and frightened to pieces. I hope you took him quick."

On February 15, 1982, the *Ocean Ranger* sank on the Grand Banks. Eighty-four men died that night. Brendan Marsh went down with the rig. But before he died, thought Janice, he helped me make her, and he gave her the grey eyes that look at me with such impatience. When Janice read the reports into the sinking, they said that the waves that night were as high as eighty feet and the wind came at the drilling rigs at ninety-one knots an hour. Supply ships were ordered to stand by each of the three rigs in the area. The *Seaforth Highlander* came into range of the *Ocean Ranger* at two in the morning, and by that time, they could see that there were lights in the water, attached to floating life preservers. They had tried to pull in the lifeboat, the one with a hole on the bow on both sides, but it slipped out of their grasp, capsizing as the men rushed up to the gunwales. Once in the water, they were unable to grasp the lines that the supply ship put out to them, or to board the life raft that it launched. God let it have been fast, Janice thought. She wondered if Brendan had made it into that lifeboat, if he thought in that moment, when the rescue ship put out a line to them, that he was going to live. She wondered if he thought about her and the baby who would become Bride.

The paper said that twenty-two bodies were recovered. Brendan's was not among them. The autopsy reports said that the men had died by drowning in a hypothermic state. The water temperature at the time was 0.7 degrees Celsius. The investigators were never sure of how the men left the rig, as at least one of the lifeboats was likely submerged at the time the rig was abandoned. One of the others was launched and lost in the process. Thirty or more men were in the lifeboat positioned at the port stern, the lifeboat that the *Seaforth Highlander* put a line out to.

Janice thought about these facts — water temperature, the number of lifeboats, the number of bodies — but nothing added up. I need to know what he thought. I need to know what he saw in his own grey eyes before the water went over his head. That would give me enough to know what his life meant.

A month later they located the rig by sonar. It had been crushed into the seabed and the rig was resting on its upper deck. Ships working in the area continued to pick up debris from the wreck. During the summer of 1982, two life vests marked "Ocean Ranger" were found separately on the beaches of the Faroe Islands, north of Scotland. On Orangemen's Day, 1983, a trawler pulled into port in Catalina, returning from the Banks, and surrendered a life raft from the rig to the RCMP. Janice could recite the dates, the geography, with perfect accuracy, but she could never know if his hand had grasped one of those vests, letting go as the cold took his strength from him.

∽⌒∾

"HE LIKES YOU," WANDA SAID.

She sat on Bride's bed, matching up socks from a basket of laundry.

"What do you mean?"

Bride had stopped brushing her hair. Wanda was staring at her, eyebrows raised.

"What could I mean? He's interested in you. That way. The same as they all are."

"What did he say?"

"Oh, you know, 'How old is Bride? Does Bride have a boyfriend? What's Bride like?' — all the things that they ask when they're interested."

"What do you mean, 'they?' What 'they' are you talking about?"

"Guys. When they want to screw you."

"I have no idea." Bride's mouth tightened.

Wanda turned her face away. "Bride, don't pretend. You know the way guys look at you."

Bride took the mirror off her dresser. "I can't do nothing about the way boys look at me."

"It makes the other girls jealous. That's why they hate you so much."

"They're a bunch of tits."

"Don't wave that mirror around, you'll break it." Wanda reached out and pushed Bride's hand toward the dresser. "Put it down."

"Alright."

The girls stopped talking. Bride went back to brushing her hair. Wanda got up from the bed and started flipping through the hangers in Bride's closet.

"You know what happens when you break a mirror?"

Bride did not stop brushing her hair. "What?"

"Seven years bad luck."

Bride made a small snorting sound in the back of her throat.

"It's true. You don't want your luck to change, Bride."

"You think I'm having good luck now?"

"You seem pretty lucky to me."

"Why? Because guys like to look at me?"

Wanda stopped looking through the closet. "That kind of thing will help you get out of here. It'll make it easier for you to go."

"You think I'm going out of here on my back?" Bride put the brush down on the corner of the dresser.

"I didn't mean it like that."

"What the Jesus did you mean then?"

"I meant that you can get people to do things for you. Things they wouldn't do for me."

"You want guys smirking at you all the time? Making comments as you go by?"

"They already do. But they never say nothing good." Wanda looked surprised that she had said this out loud.

Bride's voice softened. "Wanda, it don't matter what people think about you or say about you."

Wanda looked at her, shaking her head, her eyes filling up. "It does. You just haven't had nothing bad said against you yet."

Bride took the mirror off the corner of the dresser and dropped it to the floor. The silver cracked, a diagonal line running across it to the corners of the pink plastic frame.

"Mother fuck," said Wanda, staring at it. She raised her eyes to Bride.

"You make your own luck, Wanda. Now stop feeling sorry for yourself. We're going out."

∽◦∾

I KNOW SHE'S RIGHT, BRIDE thought after. I have always seen the way they look at me — that entitled look. The look that says you have something of mine, something I need. But the thing is, I like boys. Ever since I was a little kid, I always had a friend who was a boy. I could never figure out what it was that girls wanted. But guys, you always know what they want. Like Wayne. His face says just what he wants.

Bride thought about the boy, when she was eight, maybe, or nine. He had built a small lean-to behind the big hill. He had cut some small spruce and limbed them. Then he drove them into the ground and leaned them together at the top. Inside, the roots were visible in the earth and it smelled dank like a cellar. He had a fire pit, but no fire. They went there after school, around the time that the frost was coming out of the ground and the ponds and the brooks were full of meltwater. He talked about how he built his lean-to and she listened. I suppose we were playing house, Bride thought. He asked if he could look at her. She did not understand. "You know," he said, "I want to see how you're different from me."

His question was honest, with a sincerity that almost made her say yes. There was no trickery or conniving in his voice. She knew that he would have told no one. He had no ambition in him, so seeing her would not have been an achievement. But she did not do it. She did not go back. He would turn to stare at her through the window when she got off the school bus in the evenings, but he never asked why she stopped coming.

Mostly, she never thought about him. His family moved to Toronto a few years after. Sometimes, when she thought about boys though, she remembered the mechanical nature of his question — how do you work?

That's the thing about boys — they can't imagine who you might be, even if they could put you all together.

∽o∾

BRIDE AND WANDA SAT ON the big rock overlooking the pond, the sun sliding out of the sky's grasp and falling behind the hill. Wanda spat into the water and two trout breached, tricked into thinking that they might eat.

"You think about what I said?"

"Yeah."

"So?"

"So, yeah. Yeah, I think so. We could stay with my Aunt Cecilia."

Wanda put her head back, watching the clouds drift across the sky. She exhaled, almost a relief. Her voice was full of plans, but not excitement.

"When?"

"Maybe the end of the summer? I'm gonna have to talk to Mom."

"Your mother's not going to like it."

"I know. Give me some time to get her warmed-up to the idea."

"She don't even like you going to the store without her knowing. She's not going to like the idea of you going to Toronto, even if you do stay with family."

"Yeah. Well I gotta think about how I tell her."

Wanda had pulled a piece of her mud-blond hair into her mouth, chewing the end of the rolled strand.

"You going to tell Ivey and Lynfield?"

Wanda spat the hair out. The wet end of it lay against her sweat-shirt like a paintbrush tapered into a point.

"You think Ivey is going to notice that I'm gone? Dad will see I'm not there before she will."

"So you're just going to go? Take off, no warning?"

Wanda clenched her teeth. Bride could see her thinking. The tension in her jaw made the vein close to her eye darker and more visible.

"I don't see no point in telling her. She won't remember. And he'll just go drinking."

"I wish Mom wouldn't care."

Wanda turned her head away before Bride realized the sting of her words.

"Not that they don't care, Wanda. Not that. I meant that I wish Mom trusted me to be okay."

"Yeah, well I guess I'm lucky that way," her voice mean. "Lucky that they have so much trust in me."

Bride leaned closer so that her shoulder touched Wanda's. "I'm sorry."

Wanda did not pull away. "Look, I know. I know your mother's fucked up too. They're all fucked."

Wanda shifted away. "Dad," she said, taking a drag on her smoke and looking down into the puddle of water that she was dipping her shoe into. "He don't see, not just because he's blind. He don't want to know stuff."

Bride was silent, watching her smoke.

"You know how they figured out he was mostly blind? He drove Uncle Mac's old car though the Hart's barn. He missed the turn and drove straight into the barn. Dad said that when they took him to have his eyes examined, the doctor said he was legally blind. He said that he thought afterwards that maybe he didn't see so good."

Wanda smiled quickly, and then her face became serious again. "Dad's not dumb, he's just weak. I thought that he was stupid when I was a kid, but he's not. It's just that the world is a bit too much for him to admit that it's real."

"We'll go, Wanda," said Bride. "I promise."

∽◦∾

"NAN?"

Her grandmother sat in the chair in the living room, watching *The Price is Right*. She looked up when Bride walked in.

"Mom not home?"

Her grandmother shook her head. Her eyes were watery blue. It always seemed to Bride as if she might cry. Bride had never seen her cry.

"Nan, I need to ask you something."

"What, my duckie?"

Bride looked down at her grandmother's ankles, crossed and prim like a schoolgirl.

"I might need your help."

Myra's eyes narrowed a little, the softness going out of her face. "What's that?"

"Well, me and Wanda, we was talking. Wanda's thinking about maybe going away in the fall."

"Away?"

"Toronto."

Her grandmother said without her asking, "So you needs some money?"

Bride nodded.

"How's Wanda going to get any money? They got nothing to give her, Down Over The Hill don't." Her grandmother always referred to the Stucklesses as "Down Over The Hill," as if the physical space that they occupied in the world said everything about who they were.

"I don't know," Bride lied.

"You and Wanda not chasing no boys up there, are you?"

Bride turned her head away. "No, Nan. We're getting work."

Myra nodded. "That's good. There wasn't much in the way of paid work when I was a girl, you had to find someone to keep you."

"Me and Wanda don't need to be kept."

Her grandmother smiled, showing the uniformity of her false teeth. "No. No, I don't suppose you do." Bride could see something in her grandmother's eyes, some kind of secret that she couldn't share — something she wanted to tell her.

"You going to be alright up there, do you think? Away from home and all?"

Bride nodded. "I want to go."

"Not that you want to go away from here is it?"

Bride shook her head.

"Not even a little bit?"

"Well, maybe a little bit," said Bride.

"When I was a girl, I went to town. Worked as a maid in a big house on Waterford Bridge Road. Your Pop came for me, though."

"You came back to marry Pop?"

The secret came back into Myra's eyes. "I came back because my mother was sick. She died that summer. It was a hot, muggy summer, and she was up to bed and couldn't get down out of it. I spent the whole summer going up and down the stairs of our old house with jugs of water and bedclothes." The years came off her grandmother's face, and her young-girl face, the face in the photograph in the kitchen, came back to her. Her grandmother was full of expectation. "I come home that spring on your grandfather's schooner from St. John's. We were married in the fall of that year. November. Poor mother was three months in the ground, the bonfires burning out on the head the night before the wedding."

"You came home for your mother, but you stayed for Pop?"

Her grandmother reached out her thin, translucent-skinned hand and stroked Bride's knee.

"I came home because I had no people in St. John's. My people were here."

"I won't have no people in Toronto except for Aunt Cecilia. Do you think I should stay?"

Her grandmother smiled. "I learned that you bring your people wherever you go, the dead and the living." She paused and all her years came back to her. "You should go."

"But Mom ..."

"Your mom still got a few things to learn, but she'll be alright. I won't leave her alone here with Roop yet."

Bride put her hand over her grandmother's and felt the tumescent veins. Flesh of my flesh, she thought.

⌀

BRIDE WALKED DOWN OVER THE hill, and up the path to Wanda's house. Corey stood on the porch, his eyes full of tears, the collar of his shirt wet.

"What's wrong?" asked Bride.

His chest shook. "It's Cereal," he said, his small boy voice husky from crying.

"Cereal?"

He nodded and smacked his small palms together, fingers spread.

"Fish truck," he said, and ran around to the back of the house, his sobs fading with his footsteps. She went inside.

A series of cats, mostly gaunt, semi-feral tabbies wandered in and out of the Stuckless house, sleeping in dishpans and wrapped around the pots of plants that Ivey rooted and then forgot to water. And there was Cereal. When Bride opened the gate to walk up the path, Cereal would come roaring out of the house, the force of his bark and his short legs keeping him airborne. Wanda's voice would come from inside, "Get back here you little Jesus-fucker."

Wanda was standing, looking out the window toward the road. "I loved that little cocksucker of a dog, you know," she said. "And I know you wouldn't know it. He pissed me off so bad sometimes

I felt like knocking him into next week. It was them times, the times when I would stand there and ball him out and raise my hand to him and think, any other dog, dogs four times his size, would have their head down and their tails between their legs. Not Cereal, buddy. He stood his ground and stared me in the eyes."

Wanda turned around. Bride saw the heartbreak on her face.

"What happened?"

"Fish truck," said Wanda. "Down for that bit of salmon the Ivanys brought in. Wouldn't fill a quarter of the truck with that bit of salmon. I don't know why they sent such a big truck." Wanda turned away again.

Cereal's name was Corey's idea. They had come from school in the afternoon when he was a pup, before he had a name, although Lynfield, who could only hear his bark, was lobbying for King. Ivey sat in the chair next to the picture window, darning a sock without holes. Cereal had nosed and pawed the cupboards open, and attacked the contents. Puffed Wheat, Corn Flakes and Honeycomb lay scattered over the linoleum.

"Oh my blessed fuck," said Wanda, dropping her bag. "Mom, look at the Jesus mess, will ya?"

Ivey turned her head and smiled.

"Holy cereal," said Corey.

"He's friggin' killing the cereal boxes," said Wanda. Cereal stood with his forepaws on a box of Honeycomb, from which he had torn bits, growling.

"He's a cereal killer," said Corey.

So, Cereal became Cereal. Until the fish truck. Now he was one of Lynfield's rescued, lost things.

"That little cocksucking dog. That was the best thing Dad ever done, bringing him home." Bride thought, just for a moment, that Wanda might cry, but instead she lit a smoke.

"You know how Dad always says that he can never understand why people throw out such perfectly good things? Washers that can be fixed, he says, bikes that Jason and Corey could ride, but not in a straight line, clothes, good clothes, he says, with just a few rips that Ivey could mend. Well it's all garbage. Stuff that other people don't want 'cause it's no good." Wanda took a long inhale from her cigarette.

"But the day he brought home the dog, he was right. 'Who,' he said, 'who puts a half-drowned, crackie puppy in a plastic Sobeys bag and puts him in a bin?'" Wanda's eyes were full of tears now, and she looked up and pulled her eyes wide open in an attempt to keep them from spilling down her face.

"Dad, he means well. He don't understand much and he don't always get things right, but you can tell he's thinking about you after you're outta sight. Mom's not even thinking about you when you're standing right there in front of her. I don't think that cunt ever had a thought in her life."

Ivey sat in the rocking chair, her face calm and distant. "Wanda. My pill?" She asked hopefully, but as if from a great distance.

"Oh shut up," said Wanda. She did not turn away from the window. "We could all be out there, flat on the road next to Cereal, and do you think that one would notice? Not so long as there was someone to shove a pill in her."

"Oh Wanda, she's not that bad."

Wanda's face was pinched with anger. "Fuck, Bride. She didn't even know Jason got born she was so full of pills afterward. You'd think Ivey pushed her brains out through her ears instead of a baby out of her twat the way the doctors treated her."

Bride could see Wanda's shoulders rising as she spoke. "Wanda? Wanda, do you want to get out of here for a while?"

Wanda turned. "Let's go get stoned," she said, sniffing hard.

∽∘∽

IT WAS ALMOST MIDNIGHT WHEN they dropped Wanda off and watched her lope up the path toward the Stuckless's little house. The moon had come up from behind the hills, hung low and heavy in the sky.

"Did you see her go in the house?" he asked. "She's pretty high."

Bride nodded. "She's fine. Even when she's high, Wanda keeps her sense of balance."

Wayne backed the truck out of the driveway and they drove down to the beach. Pulling onto the wharf, he turned the engine off. They sat silent for a moment. The sound of the water rushing around the supporting timbers and then being sucked out as the waves retreated made Bride feel uneasy, as if the wharf could be pulled out from under them. Wayne drummed his fingers on the steering wheel, slowly tapping the roundness, sliding his right index finger around the curve of it. He was looking out over the water. They both began to speak at the same time, and after encouraging the other to continue, they became silent again.

Wayne said finally, "This place is dead. Almost all that's left are the old people. A lot of people who go away from here stay alive because they have convinced themselves that everything here is the same." He paused. "I bet you're just waiting to go too."

Bride turned to face him. "You know, I never really think about it. It's just so obvious that you can't stay here. I always assumed that I would go away like everyone else. I just don't know where yet. Wanda talks about us going to Toronto. But I don't want to just show up with no plans."

"You got any people there?"

"Nan's sister. That's it."

"What do you want to do?"

"You mean for work?"

"Well, not just work. Your life."

Bride sighed. "I don't know. I don't know what I can do yet."

Wayne smiled in the dark, his teeth whiter in the dim light. "I bet you'll do whatever you want."

She looked at him closely, probably more intensely than at any time earlier in the evening. When they had been with the others, talking and laughing outside the takeout, he was loose and easy. Now, pulled back against the car door, fidgeting with his keys, he looked nervous. His conversation was deliberate and probing, a screen inserted in front of his real thoughts. He wants to touch me, she thought. I make him nervous. He wants so badly to touch me, but he's afraid. What is it that makes him hesitate? She understood the direct approach, the sliding across the seat, hand on your thigh and lips on your neck. That was easy. Accept if you wanted it, or push and wiggle free. What do I do with this though? Should I touch him? Will that make it worse?

"It's late. I think I had better go now."

He seemed almost relieved. "Okay, it's late. I have to be out on the water with the old man soon. I'd better try to get some sleep."

They drove up the hill from the cove, all the houses dark and still, like animals hiding in the woods. The lights from the car bounced off the slate-rocked banks of the roadside and slipped between the trees.

∽○∽

BRIDE SAT ON A PIECE of driftwood that had been pulled close to the fire. She could feel the heat from the flames on the soles of her boots. She thought, my Jesus he's cocky tonight. I bet that will disappear when we're alone. He was not covert in the way he appraised her now in public, drinking her in slow, deliberate sips. His eyes left her face with a smile and they flowed down the length of her. He looked her in the face again after he had finished, not turning his head away like others had done, embarrassed and shy in their want. He was a man, not a boy. Men are not afraid to want things, she thought. And just look at him. His moustache was dark against the surprising pinkness of his lips, and the stubble of whiskers outlined his jaw. The muscles in his forearms were long and sinewy, veins visible through the paleness of his skin, but his hands were almost feminine. She noticed his long, thin fingers, the prominent joints of the knuckles. The nails, cut square, were pink and clear. Only the bumps and the scars on the skin revealed that he worked with his hands. The calluses were incongruous and drew attention to the gentleness of his hands rather than making them look hard. Is it wrong, she thought, to look at a man's hands and feel them on your skin, circling your waist? Can you fall in love with a man's hands?

He was sitting on a rock on the other side of the fire, guitar across his knees. His mouth was open, laughing. Bride stepped back from the heat and stood in the semi-darkness on the outskirts of the fire shadows. People stood around the flames, some singing along with Wayne's guitar, some talking and laughing in small huddles. She took a sip from the beer that someone had handed her.

That blood of a bitch Sheila was right in there, her hand on his knee now. She was laughing and flicking her hair over her shoulder, touching Wayne frequently but not for long. She was initiating contact and then pulling back to see if he would come after her, wanting more. Some of the other girls sat around Wayne, or stood behind him, ready to run interference if another female sought access to Sheila's target, a pack of dogs trying to tree a rabbit, the alpha female moving in for the kill. Except in this hunt, the rabbit offered up its throat willingly.

She turned her back on the fire and walked down the beach. She felt the wall of cold air as she stepped out of range of the flames. It was inky black when she looked away from the light. She walked cautiously to avoid tripping over the large stones that stuck out of the sand. Bride walked until she could hear a small stream, water pouring out of the base of the cliff and winding through the streambed it had carved out of the beach rocks. Four or five big boulders had fallen out of the rock face and lay in front of the stream. She put her hands out in front of her until she felt the rough, cold surface of a rock on her fingertips. She sat on it, climbing a little to the flat top. She zipped her jacket closed and looked up at the sky. The stars were small and cold.

Her name came out of the darkness, followed by the sound of feet on the beach. It was too dark to recognize Wayne's outline as he walked toward her. He said her name with certainty, as if he could smell her in the darkness.

"Bride?" This time his voice began to question her presence.

"What?"

"Where are you?"

"Over here. Mind the rocks."

Too late. She heard him smash a limb into a large boulder closer to the cliff.

"Holy fuck," he said. She could hear the slow, scuffing sound of him hopping on the sand.

"Come here. What did you do?"

"Holy, contemptible, despicable fuck. What do you think I did? I smashed my knee." He limped toward the sound of her voice, the beach rocks crunching under his feet, and leaned up against the rock on which she sat.

"You alright?"

He pulled up the leg of his jeans, and she heard him breathing quickly with pain. "I'm fine. What a fucking place to put a rock."

They both laughed quietly. He leaned closer to her, putting his arm around her and resting his palm on the rock.

"So, I was hoping that you might come and sing with me tonight."

"Don't sing." She turned her head away from him and looked back out to sea.

"Much rather be out on the water on a night like this than here on shore." He started the sentence quickly, moving from music to the water without connection.

He needs to keep talking, she thought. He's afraid of silence.

"When we was fishing, sometimes I would sit up on deck late, when everyone was in their bunks, and just listen to the water. It's like the tide pulls you out with it and you can just trust it to take you where you should go."

"What are you going to do now? Fishery is mostly closed. Cod fishery anyway."

"I don't know what to be doing. If I go back up to the mainland, the folks are here on their own. I've been trying to get on at Come By Chance, but nothing yet. Just helping Dad with the tourists."

He reached into his pocket. "Smoke?"

She shook her head. The lighter flared, cutting the darkness in half on either side of the flame.

"What about you? You're done school this year?"

"Yeah. I've been thinking about going to Toronto. Like I said."

He cleared his throat. She felt him move his body closer. "Bride?"

"Yeah?"

"Can I kiss you?"

She turned her head toward him. "I think you'd better."

The brush of his moustache against her lips made her feel small for a moment, and off balance. She felt him touch her hips with the tips of his fingers, as if he held a hand grenade. The height of the rock on which she sat made her slightly higher than him. She slid toward him so that he stood between her thighs, her arms resting on his shoulders.

As he pulled her into him, she thought of Wanda, of how she narrowed her left eye when she was angry. Wanda would be mad if she let this happen, Bride thought. This thing with Wayne would make Wanda nervous.

He slid his hands from her back to her ribs, let them rest below her breasts, and Wanda's angry face faded from her mind.

∽૦∾

SHE SMILED AS SHE KISSED him, and his tongue touched her teeth. In the daylight he would have seen that they were even and fair, except that the two front teeth tipped slightly inward toward each other, an imperfection in an otherwise perfect row. She brushed her lips against his, pulling up, letting them linger, motionless just for a moment.

Oh, sweet, dirty Jesus, he thought. I'm caught now. Wayne put his hands on the small of her back and pulled her into him. The pain in his knee shot up his leg in a pulsing wave. I'm in it now, he thought, and he could feel a space open up somewhere inside him.

This girl. She was full of secrets and flight. When she spoke to him, she often looked away, as if to hide something. She seemed as if she might leap each time he had tried to touch her, and so he pulled back. Then she walked away tonight and he knew she meant him to follow. She had watched him watching her, and she did not turn her head, but simply retreated. An invitation.

As he stroked her, she leaned closer, putting more of her weight onto him. This is good, he thought. Good and dangerous.

∽⚬∾

WANDA TUCKED A STRAND OF hair behind her ear and placed her hand back on the pool stick.

"Six off the cush, corner pocket."

The balls cracked together, followed by a quick thud as the six bounced off the cushioned edge of the table and spun into the corner pocket. Wanda walked to the other side of the table, squatted, and rested the butt of her stick on the floor. From this lower angle, she studied the position of the balls on the table. The boy on the other side snorted nervously and, as if to distract her, began twirling his stick in her range of vision.

"Put that stick down, Darren, or I'll beat the piss out of you."

He stopped. Wanda's eyes never left the table as she spoke. She was silent for a few more moments and then, calling her shots, she quickly pocketed two more balls, including the eight. Wanda scooped the money on the side of the table and nodded at Darren.

"Nice to take some money off ya there, buddy."

She walked away from the table and stood in the doorway of the takeout. She pulled her jacket close around her, making the smallness of her frame visible. She sized-up the gravel parking lot — four pickups with a bunch of stragglers hanging about the windows. From where she stood on the porch, she could see the baseball caps interspersed with the heads of girls. She looked for money. Who was going to have dollars to deal tonight? Not a lot of transactions here, she thought.

The older teenagers sat in their cars drinking beer, the passenger side doors close to the woods and the windshield pointing toward the road that led into the cove. Any sight of the RCMP's ghost car and the case of beer went into the woods under the arm of the guy closest to the door.

Bride and Wayne were nowhere to be seen. They had dropped Wanda two hours ago and disappeared up Big Pond Road. Parking. The boys had hooted and snickered about that.

"He think he can get anything off her?"

Colin sighed. "Well, he might not, but if it was me, I'd die trying, let me tell ya." He made breast-shaped cups of his hands again, as he always did when Bride was mentioned, and licked his lips.

"She don't put out," Leroy stated flatly, knowingly. "She'll play a little bit, but not all the way."

Colin snorted. "So she didn't put out for you. Who would? That don't mean she don't want some, if you got a lot to give." Colin gripped his crotch. "She wants to make it worth her while, buddy."

There was a little appreciative laughter as Leroy's mouth went tight.

"She's not with Wayne because of his gear. She's with him because he got his old man's truck. Girls cares more about stuff than skin."

Vincent spoke. He had been looking down the road, smoking, as if he were ignoring the boys.

"You two don't know nothing about women. All you know is what you can see in the shape of their tits and asses. I doubt that either one of ya have ever been up close and personal with pussy." His voice was without humour.

Colin responded slowly, cautiously. "So tell us, Vincey. Tell us about all the quality time you spend with pussy."

"Well, that would be a mistake right there, little man. Girls like secrets. Especially about sex. Make a girl feel like she's better than the other ones, prettier, and that she can trust you and you'll be too tired to jerk off at night. She'll give you anything you want."

"Anything?" said Colin. "Not just pussy?"

Leroy snorted. "What else can you get off a girl except pussy?"

Vincent looked around. Wanda was making a deal on the side of the takeout that backed onto the woods. "Some girls got stuff more important than sex to offer," he said. "Sometimes you got to be the whore." He put his hands in his pockets and walked away without speaking to the others.

Leroy laughed. "He's fucked, hey? Like there is anything more important than pussy."

Colin sighed. "You know, sometimes he gives me a bad feeling in my guts. Like I have to take a shit."

∾o∾

"WHY NOT?" WAYNE SAID, HIS eyebrows pulled together.

She looked away. She pressed down the seam on the leg of her jeans with her index finger, studying the stitching. "I just can't."

"Your mother won't let you go?"

She looked up and stared out at the pond through the windshield of the truck. "Well, she wouldn't like it."

"You don't have to tell her."

"Yeah, well, I just don't think this is a good idea."

The moon had come up and hung heavy over the pond. The water moved in waves toward them as the wind pushed it, black ripples moving quickly. Wayne shifted so that his body was closer to Bride, sliding out from behind the wheel. He raised his arm, hesitating before touching her hair, then letting his hand cup the back of her head.

"So soft," he said, as if to himself. "Blacker than bottom in twenty fathoms of water." His fingers drifted down to the skin of her neck.

She inhaled and pulled her head away, then turned it to speak. His smile was sweet, making her ache for the taste of him on her tongue.

"I think we'd better go get Wanda."

"Now?"

"Yeah. She'll be pissy with me."

"She'll be alright. She'll get a ride home with someone else."

"She won't go home without me." He is bullying me, she thought, bullying with smiles. And he doesn't think I know. I wonder how stupid he thinks I am.

Wayne sighed and started the truck.

"You're the boss," he said.

So, Bride thought, that's what he wants me to believe. I'm in charge. That's his opening move.

∽∘∾

VINCENT WALKED ACROSS THE PARKING lot of the takeout, his feet disturbing the gravel as little as possible. He did not walk with the heavy, random tread of the other boys, but picked his way delicately, navigating the straightest, surest path. He had a lightness and agility in his step so that, rather than making him seem feminine as a more slender boy might appear, he looked more powerful, more determined and somewhat unpredictable. He was tall with soft brown hair that waved in a dip at the front, despite the application of gel to separate and raise the strands. His eyes were small almonds, brown and deeply set, so that people felt that they had to lean close to really see him.

The other boys called him Vincey in an attempt to make him familiar, chummy. He encouraged the camaraderie of other boys. Vincent spent time fishing or cutting logs. He did things that required the collective strength of men, not because this is how things were done, but so that he could create opportunities for future favours. The time he spent alone, he played computer games in his grandmother's upstairs bedroom, where he had lived since his mother moved to Vancouver, speaking only to the old woman when absolutely necessary. She was mostly deaf and did not notice the silence.

The computer was the principal's old machine, which he had agreed to exchange with Vincent in return for cleaning up the barn that sat on the edge of his property. Vincent contracted out the work to four younger boys of fourteen — big enough in body to do the work, but limited enough in experience not to expect much in return. At the end of each day he paid them each six beers, which was enough to make them drunk without making them too sick to work the following day. He had quietly stolen the beer in small batches from the cold room of the Marsh's store. It took him three weeks to acquire the capital to finance the computer deal.

He had watched Wanda and Bride earlier in the evening. Wanda had immediately walked away from Bride when Wayne pulled into the parking lot, refusing her pleas to come with them. Instead, she walked behind the takeout with two men who had come to buy weed, leaving Bride still talking.

Vincent thought about how much he disliked Bride. Fine set of tits and a good, solid ass, but too wily. Every time she saw him she smiled and said hello, but she wrinkled up her nose like she smelled something bad. She was the kind of woman who would only be trouble.

Wanda was finishing the transaction as Vincent walked around the corner of the takeout. She looked up.

"What?"

"Hello to you too, my love."

"What the fuck do you keep hanging around me for?"

"The pleasure of your company."

"I'm not giving you no free draws, so if that's what you're thinking, you got another thought to think."

Vincent took out his cigarette pack. "Smoke?"

Wanda took one, putting it in the half-full pack in her pocket.

"I'm right hurt that you thinks that I wants free weed. Is that all you think that guys want from you?"

Wanda's eyes narrowed. "Look, my son, I don't know what your game is here, but it won't work. Don't come over here trying to charm me."

Vincent did his best hurt-dog look, opening his small eyes wide. "Wanda, you got a lot of qualities that I admire in a woman. You're direct. You know the value of a dollar. You're willing to work hard. There's no back doors with you Wanda, and that's something that I think a person should aspire to." He stopped to take a deep pull on his cigarette. "A woman is more than the sum of her parts." He stepped just a little closer to her. "Although, you got some very nice parts." He let his eyes drop to her hips. "Not all men want a fat-bottomed girl in their bed, you know."

Wanda had stopped talking now and her cheeks were starting to flush.

"Anyway, I just come over to see you. I better go." He tossed the cigarette onto the gravel, letting it smolder as he looked at her, smiling, and then started to back away.

"See ya now."

❧

IT WAS DARK WHEN THEY came back down the road to the takeout. Bride rolled down the window, letting the summer dust from the gravel roads into the truck.

"Colin?" she called across the parking lot.

Colin heard her voice and handed his beer to the boy standing next to him. "Sounds like Wayne's not enough man for that young Bride." He turned and trotted over to the truck, his arms out and bent at the elbow.

"Bride, my angel, you finally come to your senses and going to sit on my face? You name the place, my love."

"Shut up, Colin. Where's Wanda?"

"Wanda, well now, let me see. I think she might be behind the takeout. Why don't you get out and I'll go help you find her?"

Wayne jammed the truck into park and slid out from behind

the wheel. He put his arm around Bride's shoulder as he leaned to speak through the passenger side window.

"Fuck off with the bullshit, maggot. Where's Wanda?"

Colin stepped back from the truck, removing his forearm from the window edge. "I don't know. She left here walking about half an hour ago."

They left the parking lot immediately and Colin stood back, watching the truck go. One of the boys called out, "No threesome tonight, hey?"

Colin shook his head. "She has me booked for Wednesday. You gotta plan these things you know."

∽o∽

WHEN THE TRUCK ROUNDED A turn in the road, the headlights picked up her shape on the roadside, walking alone in the darkness. They pulled over ahead of her. She did not hurry up to the vehicle, but walked at the same pace up to the passenger door, opened it, and slid in next to Bride.

"Why did you leave?"

Wanda stared out into the night, not looking at her. "Nothing going on tonight. No one got any money until the cheques come out on Friday."

"But why didn't you wait for me?"

Wanda hesitated for a moment. "Who knew when you'd be back?"

Bride stopped talking. She felt Wayne's right hand rest on her knee.

"I always come back for you, Wanda."

"Yeah, well," Wanda looked down at the floor of the truck, "I just didn't know."

∽o∽

AFTER THEY HAD DROPPED HER off, Wanda walked toward the door of her house as she always did after a night of business. Like all other nights, when it looked as if she had gone inside and the lights pulled slowly out of the driveway, she jumped off the porch and ran around to the back of the house.

The outhouse leaned toward the bay. Lynfield had built it from wooden clapboard and vinyl siding that he had found in the dump, discarded from other people's renovations. The multitude of colours and textures always made Wanda think that it was a biblical shit-house, the toilet of many colours. Lynfield had hung a window at adult eye level so that sighted visitors could look down the sound when seated.

The blackness of the night made the toilet appear now as a simple, tall box. After the Stucklesses had installed indoor plumbing, it fell into disuse, providing only for emergencies. The enamel pot lids that rested on the two holes were now dust-covered, untouched since the boys were little and emergencies were frequent. Lynfield had filled much of the tiny floor space with collected discards from the dump, so that it now housed a different kind of refuse, including an old toolbox.

The step from the ground to the floor of the outhouse was high. Wanda put one foot up and used her hands on the doorframe to lever the remainder of her body into the narrow space. She let the door drop shut behind her and slid the eyehook catch into place.

It was completely dark with the door closed, as the dim light that would have shone through the window was blocked by a large piece of plywood, sawed and rejected by some carpenter. Wanda's hands knew the location of the toolbox by the feel of the books, old westerns, stacked on top of it. Their pages had expanded in the dampness, and the covers, like the open shells of clams, were pushed apart by the plump paper. She slid her hands down the pile until she felt the cold metal and lifted the lid slightly, without removing the books.

Almost one thousand dollars, she thought. She could never count the total in the dark, but she knew the amount of each deposit exactly, and by her math, she was almost ready. By the end of the summer, she could go. By September, she would be out of the cove.

꒰ঌ◦৩꒱

BRIDE WAITED ON THE FRONT porch of the house, listening to
the sound of Wanda's voice screaming at the boys to "shut the
fuck up." Forks clattered against plates as the Stucklesses ate
and shouted. The only female voice, the voice attempting to keep
order, was Wanda's. From where she sat, her feet hanging from
the side of the porch, Bride could hear the unmistakable slap of
a hand against a head and the empty air that followed it for a
moment. Then a boy started to cry — a pain-cry — and another
boy laughed. Bride heard Wanda swear again, and Lynfield's
voice said, "Now boys." Then she heard the quick footsteps in
the hallway, moving toward the door, and Wanda walked out. The
screenless storm door banged behind her.

"Fucking savages, I tell ya."

She stood on the porch, fumbling through her pockets until she
found her cigarettes. Her lighter made a scratching sound and the
hard, rough smell of tobacco hung in the air. Bride turned around.

"You ready?"

"Yeah. Let's fuck off outta here."

They walked in silence down the path to the road. Wanda smoked.
Bride watched her from the corner of her eye, seeing something take
form in her mind as they walked.

"How come Wayne didn't pick you up from home tonight?"

"He didn't because I told him not to."

They had reached the gate that opened onto the road. Lynfield
had made it from a discarded window frame. A piece of thick rope
that looped over the fence held the gate closed.

They walked in silence for a bit before Wanda spoke again.

"So what are you planning to do with Wayne?"

Bride laughed. "You mean tonight?"

Wanda did not smile. "I mean, has he asked you to stay here?
Did you tell him that we are going away in September?"

Bride lied. "I didn't tell him anything and he didn't ask me nothing."

"You're still coming with me, right?"

"Wanda, where are you going to get the money? I can ask Nan, but it won't be enough for both of us."

"I got a plan. Don't worry about me."

Bride stopped walking.

"You make enough from the weed?"

"I do alright."

They turned the corner in the road. The cove lay at the bottom of the intersecting gravel roads. The sound of motorboats echoed off the hills that surrounded the harbour.

"So why didn't you let Wayne come and get you tonight?"

Bride sighed. "Because I'm going out with you, stupid. Just because I see Wayne later in the night don't mean that I can't spend time with you."

"You don't have to spend time with me, you know. I'm not some frigging youngster."

"Oh for fuck's sake, Wanda, I didn't mean that. I meant that I'm not going to dump my best friend just because I'm going out with someone."

Wanda stopped talking.

"So will you go with me? In the fall? I have to leave." Wanda's voice was firm, not fragile-defiant, but sure of herself.

"Yeah. I'll go if we can both get the money."

∾∞∾

WANDA WAS SHOOTING POOL WHEN Vincent walked into the take-out. He left the door ajar, as if he forgot to close it when he saw her. He went and stood by the plate-glass window that provided a perfect view of the road that led out of the cove. He folded his arms over his chest and tucked his hands into his armpits, not letting them drape across the bend of his elbow as a woman would do. He pushed out his chest and stared at Wanda, his eyes following her every move, assessing each shot that she made. As she pocketed the eight and collected her bet, he walked over to her. He placed his hand on the stick she held in her hand and she looked at him with a frown.

"What are you smelling around me for? I don't give out no samples you know."

He pulled the stick out of her hand and rested it against the wall, smiling. "I can buy weed if I want, Wanda. I'm not looking for anything except you to come for a walk with me."

Wanda looked at her shoes for a moment. "I got some work to do. Talk to me later tonight."

Vincent sighed, his face full of earnest disappointment. "I'll wait, my trout," he said, letting go of her arm and walking back out though the open door, leaving it ajar.

∽◦∾

THEY WERE WALKING ALONE. WANDA put her hands in her pockets, keeping a distance between them, speeding up if Vincent stepped too close to her.

"So, you do all the looking-after of your brothers, hey? I see them come to you all the time in school."

"Well, someone got to look after the little friggers. Dad's not around too much and Ivey's never there."

"You call your mother Ivey?"

"Yeah."

"How come?"

"You only call mothers, mom. She's never done nothing to act like a mother."

"Yeah, well my mother took off a few years back. She calls sometimes, but it's not like she's coming back or nothing." He paused and looked at the ground for effect. He felt Wanda slow down and he drifted a little closer to her.

"Some women make lousy mothers," said Wanda.

"Yeah, well, I'm not going to be sitting around moaning about it. I'm going to get outta here and she never needs to hear tell of me again." He paused again. "Of course, I'll let Nan know where I am.

She's pretty much raised me." He remembered to seem grateful.

He could feel Wanda become more interested as he spoke. The distance that she had maintained between them lapsed to almost nothing.

"Where you planning to go?"

"I got an uncle in Fort McMurray. I might go there to start, try and make some money quick."

"I'm going to Toronto," Wanda said. Her voice was full of confession.

Here we go, thought Vincent. "How you going to get the money to go?"

Wanda hesitated. "I got a plan," she said quickly, walking faster.

Shit, thought Vincent. Women are hard work.

∽੦∾

BRIDE ASKED HER POINT-BLANK, without any subtley. "Are you going out with Vincey?"

"Are you fucking nuts?" Wanda's head snapped around. "Who told you that?"

"I seen you two walking together."

"Well, I can't stop the cocksucker from walking down the same road as me."

Bride hesitated for a minute. "You need to watch out for him. He's not a nice guy."

"Why do I need to watch out for him? I'm not going out with him."

"Well, I'm glad to hear that."

"I bet you are. You wouldn't like it if I had someone too."

"What do you mean?"

"Bride, you got Wayne, and you got me to hang out with when Wayne's got no time for you. You wouldn't want me to have some-one too."

"I can't believe you just said that. What a miserable thing to say. I think you're jealous."

Wanda made a snorting sound. "Why would I have anything to be jealous about? You got some opinion of yourself." She trailed off, hurt creeping into her voice.

"You don't have to hang out with the likes of him, Wanda. You can do better than that. He's using you."

"You don't think Wayne is using you? You think if you didn't look the way you do he'd have anything to do with you?"

"Fuck off about the way I look."

"Well, you fuck off about Vincent."

They stood in silence for a moment, facing each other.

"I gotta go," Wanda said, and turned to walk away.

Bride watched Wanda, seeing how the anger made her limbs stiffer, her motion less fluid. I swear to God that some men can smell vulnerability, she thought. Vincent has that kind of nose. A nose for weakness. They can smell it off a girl the same way that dogs smell a bitch in heat. Of course, most times men don't even know what they smell. It's not like they sit around on the tailgates of their pick-ups thinking, why can I not stop staring at the way that girl's T-shirt pulls tight across her breasts. They just follow their noses.

∽○∽

HOME IS THE PLACE YOU hide from, Bride thought, adjusting the baggy sweatshirt so that it covered the low rise of her jeans. Her makeup was at Wanda's. Tonight she would stand in front of the highboy with the small mirror that had lost much of its silver, cloudy and tarnished at the edges. She would open her mouth as she put on mascara and eyeliner, loosening her lips into a full pout for the lip gloss. Janice would have nothing to comment on if she did not see her made-up face.

Her mother's back was turned to the kitchen as she wiped the spills off the white range. The television was loud in the living room, and Bride knew from the silence that Roop was asleep. She imagined his fingers, fat and short, losing their grip on the brown bottle. He would be up late tomorrow morning, walking around the kitchen, scratching his chest and belching silent belches that made his stomach pull up like a cat about to vomit. I wish he'd just burp out loud, she thought every time she saw the contortions of his stomach fat, flung upward by the compression of internal air.

Roop snored, more like a snort, which brought him back to consciousness. The vibrations in his nasal cavity must have shaken his brain awake. He yawned. Loudly. Everything that Roop did was loud — eating, yawning, scratching, farting. Everything except burping. Roop tried to burp with restraint, but he did not have the body type for it. The mound of fat on his abdomen convulsed.

The yawn made Janice turn, breaking Bride's path across the kitchen with her stare.

"You going out with Wanda?"

Bride nodded.

"That Wanda stays out late. I don't like you to be out that late." Her mother looked at her from the floor up, then down again.

Bride spoke without looking at her mother. "Like I said, if I don't wait for Wanda, I got to walk home by myself."

"Well, I don't want you to walk across the island by yourself. Can't you find someone else to walk home with?"

Bride looked up. "Mom, none of the other girls are supposed to be home by eleven."

Janice's mouth tipped down at the corners. "Just remember, I'll find out if you were up to something. I'll hear about it."

No, thought Bride, as she tied her shoes. No, you most certainly will not.

∽o∾

JANICE COULD HEAR THE REGULAR vibrations of the snore again, ripping a hole in the television laughter. He would be asleep until eight or so, and then he would be gone to the Cariboo. Her hands moved in circles, her fingernails scraping at the burnt-on particles through the cloth of the dishrag. The scratching sounds were rhythmic and regular, interrupted by snoring. Each rough intake of his breath made her hold her own just a little.

He started awake again. The vinyl of the recliner squeaked as he pushed himself out of it.

"Mother of fuck," he said yawning. "Any supper?" He scratched the back of his head and smiled. "Any supper, my love?"

She pulled a covered dish out of the oven. He was sitting at the table when she turned with the warm plate in both hands. As she put it in front of him, he slid his hand across the back of her thigh. "Come up to the club. The other women will be there on Saturday night."

She brushed his hand away with the potholders. "Rupert," she said, her voice tired with past explanations and spent patience. "Rupert, I'm driving to church tomorrow, so don't bring the car home full of beer stink. It's my turn to drive Mom and Mrs. Snelgrove."

He held the handle of the fork in the junction between his thumb and forefinger, flat against his palm. His elbow was on the same plane as his wrist as he pushed the potato into his mouth. Rupert's large white teeth chewed as he spoke.

"Right. No beer in the car. You got any money?"

"You know I do."

"Well, give me some then."

Again, Janice's voice seemed to tire. "Rupert, you drinks some pile of money."

"Not half as much as you gives to Jesus. At least your money makes me happy. All the money that you gives to the Salvation Army goes to drying people out, making them unhappy. How come no one ever started a church to encourage people to drink, be happy?"

"Not everyone finds that being drunk makes them happy."

"Well, my dear, that's a psychological problem that money should be spent on. You find a church that is willing to devote themselves to researching how to make people happy drunks and I'd give them money."

"Rupert, you don't make any money."

"Well, that's why you should give me some. A man with a bad back and all."

Janice took out her wallet. Small price to pay, really.

∽∽∾

BRIDE PULLED THE SHIRT OVER her head. It was yellow, Wanda's favourite colour. The fabric pulled taut across her breasts.

"You're going to have all my shirts stretched to pieces."

"I won't wear it if you don't want me to."

"Nah, it's alright. It goes back in shape when I wash it. Gimme that lip gloss."

Bride threw it across the bed so that it landed in Wanda's lap.

"Since when do you wear lip gloss?"

"Since now." Wanda plunged the brush in and out of the tube of pink.

"Wanda, don't be mad, but what about this Vincey business?"

The brush made a plop as Wanda pulled its tip from the tube. "What about nothing. There is nothing to 'what about.'"

"Wanda, you're wearing lip gloss."

Wanda was standing now, rubbing the brush hard across her thin lips, making the bristles spray out and concentrate the colour at the edge of her mouth.

"You the only one who can wear makeup?"

Bride knew that Wanda was seeing her reflected in the mirror even if their eyes did not meet. "I said don't be mad. I'm just a bit worried."

"I can look after myself. I don't need the likes of you to do it. You should worry about yourself. Worry about Wayne sniffing up your skirt."

Bride felt the tightness of the T-shirt across her back and the smallness of the cap sleeves as they cut into her arms.

"You know, maybe this shirt doesn't fit me after all." She stood and pulled it up from the waist. As she struggled to pull the thin yellow fabric over her head, she could see that Wanda had put down the lip gloss and was looking at her breasts.

"Can I look for another one?" she said, opening the dresser drawer.

"Yeah," said Wanda. "This lip gloss tastes like shit."

❦

MYRA SAT IN THE FRONT seat of the Neon, her purse on her lap. Her daughter's body leaned into the back seat. The smell of Mr. Clean fighting with the smell of stale beer vomit became stronger as she scrubbed.

"You can hardly smell it now, Janice. Come on, we'll be late."

"Mrs. Snelgrove can't sit back here in this state." Myra could feel how angry her daughter was from the vigour of her scrubbing. How can so much anger go into cleaning? Maybe that's why we are always at it, the never-ending scrubbing. If we didn't have nothing to clean, all the women would be in jail and all the men would be run over with these little japanesy cars they sells these days. At least in my day they had them big heavy cars, like that old blue Pontiac we had. I could have done her father with one swipe. In this little thing, she'll have to reverse over Roop two or three times to finish him off. Blessed Jesus. She stopped the scene of Roop's murder from playing any further in her mind. This is what happens to you when you gets old. You lets your mind think all kinds of things that you can't think when you're young and strong enough to act on them.

"Janice, maid, come on."

The back door slammed. Janice sat behind the wheel, her face a sheet of ice.

"Now you enjoys Army, Janice. Don't let this take all the joy out of the morning for you."

"He does this every Sunday morning."

"Well, then don't give him your car."

Janice turned on the windshield-washer fluid to clean the bug-splattered window.

"He's my husband."

"Well, you can fix that right quick nowadays." You can fix it without having to even start your car now, she thought. All done on paper. No mess.

"Mom. He's good to Bride. Brendan would have wanted her to have a father who was good to her."

"Brendan is dead. But you're not. You got to suit yourself."

Janice stopped talking. They drove out around the harbour in silence, except for the country music on the radio. Man, I feel like a woman, Shania sang. Frigging right, thought Janice.

"He's her uncle you know. It's not so surprising that he is good to her, loves her."

Janice looked into the rearview mirror, no other vehicle behind them on the empty Sunday road. Nothing following her.

"That's what I was counting on. That he would love her."

∽∘∾

RUPERT HEARD THE CAR DOOR slam and his first thought was, mother of fuck. The vomit. I was supposed to clean up the vomit.

As she pulled the car out onto the road, the sand on the drive-way sprayed out from the back tires and hit the fence. Women. They won't say nothing to you, but they'll stand on the accelerator like it was your neck under the heel of their shoe. She'll have her mouth all down around her ankles now for days. His wife's mouth was always turned down. He married a sad woman. Maybe that's why he did it. He wanted to kiss all the sexy sadness out of that mouth. When Bride was small, Janice would stand in the window, looking down the sound, and rock her to sleep with the swaying of her body, her mouth pouting like she was about to cry. He would take her to bed later in the night and rock her and stroke her and bite her until she cried out, but it always sounded like a pain-cry to him, a release of hurt. Now? No touching, no release.

He rolled over and his eyes bounced back hard against his brain. Enough of this foolishness, he thought. I might as well get up.

❦

BRIDE HEARD ROOP PISSING IN the toilet. The head of her bed rested against the bathroom wall. Roop pissed loud too. But before he pissed he would inhale, pulling the snot out of his sinuses, down to the back of his throat, and spit into the toilet. "Horking up a big lubbie," he called it. Lubbie horked, he would proceed to piss. The sound of urine hitting the water made her own bladder ache. She waited for the force to subside to intermittent dribbles. Then he farted — a loud, long, whiny fart. He flushed.

Roop. Bless his heart, as Nan said when he broke one of the teacups that her mother had given her, crumpling it in his big paw. "Sorry, Nan," he would say, and flash his big white teeth at her. Bride never called him Uncle. Just Roop. Her mother called him Rupert, as if by stating his full name she could civilize him.

When Bride asked about her father, her mother's response was always the same.

"He was nothing like Rupert."

When she was a child, she would think about how Brendan died. This seemed to make sense to her when she was little. In the month of February, most things are just one false step from death — that is, anything that is still alive. She would sit in the big rocking chair in the winter and watch the bare branches of the lilac tree, coated with ice, struggling to bear the weight of winter, and think, that's it, it's not going to make it through this one.

She thought about Janice, sitting on the wharf, watching the ice break-up in the sound. Nan said she spent most of that spring just sitting there, looking out the arm, or wandering the beach. Anytime I was sleeping, Mom was down there looking for him, I guess. I wonder if she thought that when the ice melted, the body would wash up on shore. Maybe she thought that the sea would give him back.

You don't get things back once they are taken from you. She imagined Janice that spring, walking the beach, hands in her pockets, kicking at the dried kelp, looking for some memento of him. Maybe his watch. Or a fragment of clothing. A boot. Always dreading to find his frozen body behind a pile of driftwood.

The screen door slammed. He was out walking on the back porch now. The thud of the rubber boots on the planking was soft, almost hollow. She heard him hork again, spitting out into the backyard this time. At least he doesn't piss out there, she thought.

Poor Rupert. Poor old Roop.

∽◦∾

JANICE WAS STOCKING SHELVES. CAMPBELL'S vegetable soup, Libby's baked beans. Crackers. Her hands moved repetitively in and out of the shelves, dry and dusty. The skin on the back of her hands was starting to lose its suppleness and she could see that the miniscule folds had deepened. Thirty-five. Thirty-five years of looking at her hands, and for the first time, she saw how they would get old — folding, puckering and becoming almost translucent. How few useful things I have done with these hands, she thought. How few people I have touched. And now I'm too old.

She placed a tin of green peas on the front edge of the shelf, lining up the label so it was centred. The smallness of the thing, its unimportance, made her eyes fill with tears so that she had to look up to keep them from spilling down her face. For the first time in a long time, she let the thought bubble up into her mind, where it hung, heavy and hard. Lonely. I'm so lonely. She thought it first and then said it to the shelf.

She knelt there, feeling disconnected and airy. After Brendan died she felt like a balloon, floating and swaying and not being connected to anything. Not being connected to anyone. Especially not Rupert.

Move the hands and the mind thinks it's busy. Stay busy and you think less. Own your own store and you have no time to think. Janice started to reach into the open cardboard box next to the shelf for another can when she realized that she still held one.

I wonder if it's possible to fill up your life with the small things, she thought. I wonder if it's possible to find enough small things to take the place of love.

∽o∾

IT WAS LATER IN THE evening when she found the cat. A wind blew down from the hills, out of the woods. It smelled of evergreen and moss and of hay fields beginning to dry. Janice rolled her sleeves up as she walked, and the warm breeze lifted the hair on her arms, as if in excitement. The day had been bizarrely calm, the sea so flat that it looked as if it would not ripple if it were touched, as if it were solid. Now this soft wind toyed with it, moving it sideways.

The cat was standing under a fish stage. He was small and orange. He held one paw off the ground and mewed, his eyes searching for some kindness in her. Janice stopped and squatted. He put the paw on the ground to walk, but withdrew it quickly as he put the first tentative weight on it. She reached her hand slowly under the stage, picking him up from under his belly. His body stiffened and he pulled his head back to look at her face. They observed each other for a moment while she stroked his ears with her free hand, feeling some of the tension leave the small body. A tiny tremor began in his chest that was the start of a purr.

She looked up the bank that ran down to the beach. On the top was an old saltbox, one of the last ones standing that had not been renovated. The teacher's house. Katie's house. She started up the hill, holding the cat close, wondering to herself why she did this, why this seemed like the right thing to do.

When Katie opened the door, her eyes met Janice's fleetingly, before pulling the cat gently, but firmly, from her grasp.

"How did you get out?" she said, speaking to the cat.

"His paw is hurt," said Janice, following Katie as she went inside to set him down on the kitchen table, brushing away the supper things with her free arm.

"It's his right front paw," Janice said, as she stood behind the chair where Katie sat facing the cat.

Katie lifted the paw and the cat flinched, but did not show its claws. She spoke softly as she stroked the cat's head with one hand and held the damaged paw with the other. It's like a child for her, thought Janice.

"There's my good boy, Hector. Just let me see what's happened." She turned the paw slightly. A small fish hook was embedded in the soft pink flesh of the pad.

"Get me the pliers. They're in my toolbox on the top shelf in the pantry."

Janice obeyed. Katie's voice had a tone, a confidence in it that raised no questions. She saw the red tin toolbox beside a collection of kerosene lamps. The cat made a cry and Janice's hand jumped as she reached up to the shelf, pushing the lamps together so that the glass shades touched and resonated a sound close to the pitch of the cat's mew. She steadied her hand and pulled the toolbox down.

Katie was standing next to the table, the cat jammed under her arm. She bent over it so that her hair fell forward, partly obscuring her view. She had pushed the barb clear so that it protruded from the top of his paw pad. The cat struggled to pull away.

"Can you hold him?" she said, not looking up. "This will just take a minute."

Katie took the pliers that Janice offered and snipped through the hook, the barbed tip falling on the table. She dropped the pliers and quickly pulled the hook back through the paw and out of the flesh.

"Now get a cloth and a bowl and put some salt water in it."

When Janice returned to the table with the bowl, Katie bathed the paw as the cat wiggled in Janice's hands. The salt would clean, but it would also sting. The wound was not deep and there was little blood. When Katie released him, he carefully jumped from the table and hid under the stove.

Janice looked around the room for the first time since entering. The big wood stove in the corner was cool and silent. A long couch lay against the wall, under the windows that looked out over the cove. The kitchen table stood in the middle of the room, but it did not make the space feel crowded. A door off the kitchen led to a living room. Katie's house was silent. A book lay open on the table and a half-cup of now-cold tea sat next to it. A butter dish, a sticky marmalade bottle and an old plate trimmed with worn gold edging sat on a placemat next to toast crumbs, piled in a heap, as if Katie was about to push them into her hand from the mat. Through the door to the living room, Janice could see bookshelves, a stereo and a large chair covered in a blanket.

When she followed Katie into the house, Janice saw the framework of the rooms and the details of Katie's life, but she had somehow overlooked the cats. All of her attention had been focused on the injured one. Now she noticed the others. A large black cat sat on the couch in the kitchen, tucked behind some pillows. Another lay on the seat of one of the kitchen chairs under the table. A third peeked out from behind the curtains, perched on the windowsill.

Katie came back to the room, wiping her hands distractedly on her thighs. "Thank you so much. It would have been so hard to get that hook out without someone to hold him. I don't know how he got out. Where did you find him?"

"He was down by the bank, the one that the boys fish off, so I guess he stepped on the hook down there. I wasn't really sure that he was yours — just a guess, really."

Katie laughed. It sounded like a small glass bell, fragile but clear. She turned, still laughing, and went back to the kitchen. Then Janice heard water splash against tin as Katie filled the kettle, her voice raised to speak over the running water.

"Even if he wasn't mine, I'm glad you brought him to me. People drop their unwanted cats here all the time. I can usually find homes for the young ones, but I keep the old cats and make sure that their last days are as good as possible. Only trouble is that I'm always losing one of them, and that's hard. But I figure I give them the best that I can. Sometimes doing the right thing is hurtful to you, but not doing it would be more hurtful to someone else."

Katie sat down at the table and waited for the kettle to boil. Janice removed her coat and sat back on the couch, stroking the black cat that narrowed its eyes at her in pleasure as she touched his tattered ears.

"He was quite a scrapper in his days as a tom. Now he's retired."

The kettle whistled and Katie went back to the pantry to fill the cups.

"So, how is Bride? Milk and sugar?" She put more air behind her voice again so that Janice could hear her as she spoke from the kitchen.

"No, black tea for me. You teach her this year?"

"She wasn't in my class. But you remember I taught her English in grade ten. Smart little girl. What's she going to do now that she's graduated?"

Janice looked at the shape of Katie standing, pouring the tea out of the pot, her back to the kitchen. She was short — her head of blonde curls not even close to the bottom of the cupboard set above the sink.

"I don't think she has her mind set on anything at the moment."

Katie returned holding two steaming mugs of tea. She handed one to Janice, then leaned one arm on the back of the couch as she squeezed herself in beside Janice and a big grey tabby that leaped up as Katie prepared to sit. Katie left her arm on the couch so that she could have touched Janice's shoulder if she stretched a bit.

"I guess she'll have to sort herself out before the end of the summer," Katie said, blowing on the surface of the liquid.

I don't remember her being so beautiful, Janice thought.

Katie began to talk again. She spoke as if no one had listened to her in a long time. Her voice was breathy, and she barely paused between sentences. She asked few questions, but spoke in an earnest voice about the house, her garden and school, her eyes never leaving Janice's face.

Janice nodded, saying nothing. Her lips were hot against the ceramic mug and she thought, please don't let her stop. She became aware that she was no longer listening to the meaning of the sentences. Each individual word seemed so clear and perfect that the sounds distracted her from the connections made between them. Janice watched Katie's lips forming each word, reading them as if she could not hear her at all.

Her lips stopped moving, resting together so gently that Janice could almost feel the softness of them. Katie's eyes blinked slowly and purposefully, as if each movement were a conscious, thoughtful act. A sprinkle of freckles fell across the bridge of her nose and dusted the tops of her cheekbones. The skin was pale, but not transparent and bluish like Janice's. The pink tint of her face was enhanced by the blondness of her hair.

Janice felt as if an electric current pulsed through her, as if she were becoming the conductor for all of Katie's energy.

She stood up, gripping her jacket in one hand.

"I have to go, Katie," she said setting down the teacup on the kitchen table. She did not trust her eyes to find the physical space that the table occupied. She touched it with her hand to be sure the table was real before letting go of the handle of the cup.

Katie stood and stepped closer as Janice bent her head to zip her jacket. She put her arms around Janice and settled her lips on her cheek. She whispered in her ear, "Thank you. Thank you for bringing him back."

Janice's arms remained at her sides. She stepped back, the outlines of the doorframe blurring.

"No problem."

The screen door banged shut behind her. As she started to walk down the hill, she felt a watery sensation in her belly. She turned and looked back up the hill. Katie's face looked out from the window, one arm holding back the curtains, another holding the small orange shape of the cat.

∾○∾

RUPERT HEARD HER IN THE kitchen sometime around three, the fridge door opening and the kettle being filled. She was sitting at the table drinking tea when he got up. She pulled the bathrobe tight around her and crossed her legs.

"She not home yet?' he said looking at the clock. It was twenty-eight minutes after three.

Janice shook her head, her bottom lip pinched tight between her teeth. She looked down into her teacup.

"Don't worry, she's with Wanda probably. Know where they are?"

"They went to a bonfire I think."

"Down on the beach?"

"I suppose. I think they know better than to set a fire in the woods this time of year."

"Well, I'm going to go down there and get her. She can't have you up all night like this."

Janice looked up. Her eyes lost their faraway look and suddenly focused. "I don't want you to do that. Besides, I'm not up worrying about her. I just can't sleep, that's all."

"What can't you sleep about? What have you got to worry about?"

Janice folded her arms tighter. She looked toward the window. "Well?"

"I'm thirty-five years old. I own a grocery store. I have no life."

"Right. So what is there to worry about? You got no money problems. Your mother will give you money if you want it. She don't spend none of her pension cheque."

"Never mind." She picked up the full cup of tea and poured it down the sink. Janice walked down the hall to her bedroom, bare feet on the carpet. Rupert watched her go. Twenty to four. Might as well have a cup of tea and a smoke. It would be getting light soon.

☙❧

WANDA WAS DRUNK. BRIDE WATCHED her from across the fire — her balance and her actions betrayed nothing, but her speech was slurred a little and had slowed down. She laughed more and she touched people — sharp little punches to the shoulders of the guys she was smoking with. Wanda never touched people.

Wayne was strumming a guitar that no one was really listening to. Bride leaned over and whispered in his ear, "I have to pee."

"You want me to come with you?"

"Nah, I'll be right back."

Wayne smiled. "I could come help."

Bride tilted her head to the side. "I have been managing to do this by myself for a long time now."

"Just being thoughtful," he said, looking back at the guitar. As he played with the chords to "Out on the Mira," a girl's voice picked up the song.

Most of the stages were closed up, some starting to sag in the middle and drop toward the water as the wood aged and slackened. Only the smokehouse seemed to be perfectly preserved. Bride could smell it in the dark and knew that she was close to the path that ran up from the beach. She stopped and put her hand on the side of it, feeling for the corner. The fish oils had seeped into the wood and made it feel greasy to the touch. She turned toward the woods as she came around the corner of the smokehouse, the sound of voices fading behind her. The path was narrow and had begun to grow in at the sides. She lifted her feet carefully to avoid roots and small stones. There were lengths where the path ran close to the cliff and she ran her hand along the exposed rock like it was a lover's hip, her fingers lightly searching out the shape. The path seemed to brighten as the trees thinned ahead of her. Moonlight came out from behind a cloud, but the moon itself stayed hidden.

The sawmill was in front of her, its unpainted siding of rough-dressed clapboard silvery, the threads of the wood soft like a spider's web. The mounds of sawdust around the mill were like snowbanks, some moulded into the bottom of the cliff. The earth began to feel soft under her feet. Years of sawdust had mingled with the dirt, making it spongy.

Two rooms of the mill met in a corner, dark and private. She dropped her jeans quickly. The night air felt damp on her ass. How nice it feels to pee outside, she thought. I feel free. The sound of the water on the soft sawdust was almost silent. She rested her arms on her knees, moving her feet far apart. She remained squatted after she had finished, remembering that she had no tissues. The coolness of the night air was almost arousing. Bride thought, perhaps I should take all my clothes off and just stand here. I have never been naked outside before. Then she thought, I must be drunk.

She heard the dull sound of feet on the path, stumbling, and then a girl's laugh — a harsh, drunk, too-loud laugh. Wanda, thought Bride. She pulled her jeans up quickly, putting her hand over her zipper to hide the sound. Wanda stumbled into the clearing near the mill, with Vincent at the end of her arm.

"You're going to get what you been looking for, my son."

Vincent seemed to be pulling back from Wanda as she tugged him forward. She fell against the side of the mill, into shadow. Bride could only see Vincent now, his arms extended, holding Wanda. She saw her arms reach out of the dark to push him back, then heard a rustling and saw the flame as Wanda lit a joint.

Vincent took the joint from Wanda's pinched fingers and inhaled. Wanda spoke with held breath, not wanting any of the smoke to escape before she had to breathe again. It made her voice nasally.

"That's my private stock there buddy. I don't even sell that. I smokes my better customers up with it sometimes. I got to beg Levi for it." She exhaled and coughed from deep in her lungs.

"It's not gentle, but it is the best stone you will ever have. None of that wheelchair, BC hydroponic weed that just paralyzes you.

This is a total head stone. You gonna laugh your arse off." She began to giggle. Vincent lost the breath that he had been holding, snorting the smoke out of his nose. Wanda's giggles became full belly laughs. They built on each other's hysteria until Wanda's laughing became silent, accompanied by the smack of her hand against the mill.

Fuck, thought Bride. I can't exactly walk out there now.

"Come sit here," said Vincent, pulling her out of the shadow to an old bench embedded in the sawdust.

Vincent put his arm around Wanda's shoulders as she leaned into him. They giggled again.

"You know, this is nice weed my ducky, but that's not what I was looking for."

Wanda pulled her head back. "What?" she said.

"I said, I wasn't looking for the weed."

"What the fuck do you want then?"

"This," he said, and he took the narrow, bony edge of Wanda's jaw in one hand and pulled her face toward him. Wanda folded into him. Bride could hear the soft rustling of hands on clothed bodies.

Bugger, bugger, bugger, thought Bride. Oh bugger me.

∽o∾

THEY WERE NOT ON THE beach. The remains of the bonfire, charred wood, torn beer cases and scattered empties, was all that was left of last night's party. The tire tracks in the sand indicated that there had been vehicles down here. Rupert removed some of the sand that covered the fire with his boot. At least they had the good sense to bury the coals, which still burned under the grey and purple sand. The light was just coming onto the land, the morning still full of shadow. A light fog lay on the water, which softly slapped at the poles of the wharf and the stages spread out along the beach. Only three boats tied up to the wharf, and they were not going to be on the water today. Not too much fog, though. Probably means the capelin will be later this year. No fog, no capelin. The sun was over the hill now. Within an hour it would burn the fog off the water. He turned and walked back up the hill out of the cove.

The hill led up to the houses, mostly empty. He cut through a path between two gardens until he came on the old road, the one that they had started to build in the sixties, the one that should have reached the communities that they later resettled. They uprooted them poor people, Rupert thought as he walked down the old road, washed out in places so that he had to shimmy along the cliff and stretch over the gaps where the water took all the soil down the hillside and into the sea. And now people are uprooting themselves and going away, he thought as he looked down at the small knot of houses around the water. He came to the place where the road ended, in front of an outgrowth of rock that could neither be averted, nor blasted through. Bride was not down here. He was just wandering. The sun was well over the hills now. He stopped to look out over the cove. The grey beams of the wharf were wet with last night's dew, the sun not yet strong enough to dry it. The fog that hugged the water was almost gone and it was dead calm. Not a ripple. No wind two days in a row. It made Rupert uneasy. He listened for it, not knowing exactly what was missing. Rupert stared down at the wharf and thought of missing families. He pulled the cold morning air into his lungs and turned around, hands in the pockets of his old windbreaker. His rubber boots made a soft thump in the wet grass that had long overgrown the road as he set off down the hill.

∽◦∾

FIVE A.M. EVERY HOUR, ON the hour, Janice looked at her clock, the bright red lights reflecting her obsession back on her as she lay under the covers. She thought about the way Katie's wrist looked transparent and fragile as it lay on the edge of the couch, yet the muscles of her forearm rippled as she moved. She closed her eyes to shut out the red glare of the numbers and thought of Brendan.

She did not think of him that much anymore. She could remember only parts of him, his face mostly forgotten. I can still feel his hands, she thought. I can still feel the cup his hand made against my breast in the dark. Janice let her hands touch her own body. How would Katie's breasts feel different from mine? As different as a man's chest would feel under my hands? Her hands moved downward and she stopped herself from creating more of Katie's body in her mind.

She turned over to avoid looking at the movement of the numbers, wrapping her arms around her own body to make her feel grounded. She closed her eyes and willed her mind to stop thinking.

What foolishness, she thought. God forgive me.

∽o∾

DEREK'S CAR SAT IN A clearing in the woods that had once been a potato bed. The land was unfenced, and all around it the spruce stood black-green against a sky that was just beginning to lighten.

The car was parked with one set of tires on the top of the potato bed and the other in a trench that ran between them. The passengers in the front seat leaned toward the driver's side, the front passenger door open, legs sprawling out, running shoes in the potato mud. Wayne leaned against the window, his knees splayed under the steering wheel. Bride's head rested on his shoulder, her mouth open, neck at a sharp angle to her head. The radio had been left on. The ashtray overflowed and butts were scattered over the floor and on Bride's jeans. Wanda sat in the back seat, a half-empty beer between her thighs. Empty bottles lay in the grass. A beer case sat on the roof of the car, open so that it flapped in the wind as they drove up from the beach to the meadow last night. A pipe of clear glass lay on the dashboard, filled with sooty ash.

The angle of Bride's neck had tightened the muscles so that she thought she might not be able to move it again. Through her eyelids she could see the sunlight that had brightened the car. Someone was snoring in the back seat. It must be dawn. She smiled to herself and drifted back into the half-sleep that comes with sitting up. The last time she had seen Wanda, she had been in the back seat, wrapped in Vincent's coat. She opened her eyes and the night came back.

From where Bride had been standing, she could see that he had opened her jeans and was touching her. Wanda rocked her hips against him. They were kissing. He stopped, and even though they were alone, he whispered. Wanda moaned, and then laughed. He started to pull his hand away, but she held his wrist.

"That don't concern you. Now, never mind." She pulled his hand back toward her. "Please Vincent," she said. "Please."

Bride had never heard Wanda say please.

"You don't trust me enough to tell me a secret. We can't do this if you don't trust me."

Wanda sighed. "Vincent, this is not about nothing except what it's about." Her voice was impatient.

"I can't do this with you if you don't trust me."

Wanda had pulled his other hand forward and placed it on her small breast. He kept it perfectly still, but did not pull away. "Just touch me. Please."

"Then you got to trust me."

She put her hand over his on her chest. "I promise I'll show you later."

"Tonight?"

"Come on," she said and pressed his hand again.

He moved forward and started to touch her. She inhaled sharply.

"You promise you'll prove to me that you really trust me?"

Wanda's voice was slow and heavy with the weed. "Yes," she paused, "after."

Bride closed her eyes until the sound of their breathing made her look. Wanda was naked from the waist down, sitting on Vincent. The movement made everything clear. She wanted to look away. She watched as they finished.

Bride closed her eyes again, afraid to breathe until she heard them leave.

∽∘∾

HER HEAD WAS JOLTED SUDDENLY downward and her body seemed to follow in slow motion. When she opened her eyes she lay in the driver's seat, staring at the keys dangling from the ignition and Wayne's feet, now tangled in the pedals. Turning her head, she looked up at Rupert. Wayne lay at his feet, rubbing the elbow that he landed on when Rupert pulled open the driver's door. His hair was mussed, his chin and cheeks shadowed with stubble.

"Jesus fuck, ole man! You trying to kill me?" He looked up at Rupert from where he sat in the empty potato field.

"Well, I don't suppose you got your dick wet with that crowd in the car last night." He smiled at Bride attempting to straighten her hair in the rearview mirror.

"Get out of that car, Bride Marsh."

"Yeah, yeah, Roop. Just let me find my clothes," she smirked.

"What clothes?"

"My jacket." She started to pull it out from under Derek's sleeping body in the front seat. He murmured in discomfort and flipped over.

"You better come home right now, your mother is fit to be tied." He turned to look at the others who were roused by his voice. "And that young Wanda should be home out of it too."

"Oh, Roop," she said, pulling herself out, the jacket in one hand. "Mom's tougher than you think. And so's Wanda." From the backseat, Wanda muttered.

Bride and Rupert walked together away from the car. The sun was burning the dew from the hay in the surrounding fields, and the smell of chamomile made Bride remember tea and kitchens and how hungry she was. Wayne called out from the ground where he still sat, "Bride! I'll call ya. We needs to talk about stuff."

She turned to smile, as Rupert, pointing straight ahead, gently touched her ribs with his elbow.

꼬◦∽

MYRA AND JANICE WERE SITTING at the breakfast table when they came in, Bride first and Rupert behind her, as if to close off any escape route. Bride's eyes felt puffy. She looked at her mother and saw some of the tension go out of her face.

"Well then," she said hanging up her jacket, "time for me to be going to bed," and walked toward her bedroom.

Janice cleared her throat. "Where were you?"

Bride did not stop.

"With Wanda."

Rupert smiled. "You weren't asleep with your head in Wanda's lap when I found you."

Janice turned her head to look at him.

"Wayne," he said. "George's young fellow. Home from the mainland."

Janice called out. "Bride. If I find you hanging around with that fellow, you won't be going out with Wanda again."

Bride closed the door to the bathroom. Next time you won't find me, she thought.

"Your mother was up half the night worrying about you," Rupert yelled at her. "You got to think about your mother."

"That wasn't what I was worried about," said Janice, her finger smoothing the hair of her right eyebrow into place.

"Well, what was you so worried about?"

She looked at him. "Want a cup of tea?" she asked, as she got up from the table and turned toward the stove.

꼬◦∽

WANDA WAS STANDING WITH HER back to the path leading up to the house. She picked clothes from a turquoise plastic laundry basket — small pants and T-shirts mostly — hanging them on the clothesline. For economy, she strung the clothes together using a single pin for the shoulder of a shirt and the waistband of a pair of jeans. The line looked as if it had been strung with cut-out dolls, joined by seams of paper.

The voice from behind startled her. "Who knew you'd be such a good little housekeeper, my love?" Vincent placed his hand on the small of her back, fingertips pointing upward. He slid his thumb down her spine toward her ass. He stepped into the shape of her, moving his hand around her waist until it rested over her flat belly. As he pulled her back into him she came to life.

"What the fuck do you think you're doing?" she said, pushing his hand away and turning to face him.

Vincent now stood with his hands at his sides. "I came to see you."

"Well, I'm busy." Wanda bent to retrieve clothes from the basket.

"Too busy to talk?"

"About what?" She pulled an orange T-shirt from the basket and held it up to the clothesline.

He ducked under the wet clothes and faced her on the other side. He held her hands as she raised the shirt, bending the shoulders to pin them. Her knuckles were red and raw, as if she had scrubbed out the clothes on a washboard. Her hands were ten years older than her face.

"About last night."

Wanda let him hold the weight of her arms. "Let's sit." She gestured with her chin toward a hand-built picnic table that sat unlevelled under an apple tree. Small cars and action figures covered the table.

They sat facing outward on one bench. Wanda's arms were folded.

"So are we going out now?"

"No, we're not going out." Wanda bent forward and pulled a cigarette package from the back pocket of her jeans.

"What was that about last night?"

Wanda flicked the lighter and inhaled. The cigarette rested in one corner of her mouth. It wiggled as she spoke, making her squint with one eye to avoid the smoke. "That was pretty nice."

"So?"

"So what? I liked it. We don't have to make a big deal of it."

"So you don't want to do it again?"

"I never said that."

"It seems like you don't want to be seen with me, but you're willing to be pretty close to me sometimes." He looked into her face, trying to make eye contact as she looked past him into the road.

"Vincey, I just need my privacy."

"Even from me?"

She turned to look at him now. "What's that suppose to mean?"

He slid his arm around her. "Wanda, it hurts that you don't want people to see us together."

"I'm sitting here with you now, aren't I?"

Vincent sighed. "Tonight you'll look past me in the takeout like you never seen me before."

"Vincey, I work nights, okay?" She arched her eyebrows and slowed down the sentence, singling out the words, each of equal importance.

He sighed again. "Well, that's another thing. How come you don't trust me?"

"Are you still on about that?"

"Yeah. How can we be together if you don't tell me things? Private things?"

Wanda did not speak for a minute. "Is knowing about my business so important to you?" She stopped. "And we're not together."

Vincent put his hand on her shoulder. He made his voice soft. "Yes."

"What do you want to know?" She inhaled from her cigarette, the ash expanding toward the butt.

Vincent put his arm around her shoulders, pulling her in close. He looked out across the yard.

"Why do you do it?"

"Deal, you mean?"

"Yeah. It's a big risk."

Wanda's shoulders shook slightly as she laughed.

"I'm small fry, Vincey. A few baymen getting high is not a big deal for the RCMP. Besides, I'm pretty discrete."

"You need the money?"

"Yeah, of course I need the money. You think Oprah lives here?" She gestured toward the little house with her hand. The bedroom curtains hung out of a window at the back of the house. Two loose shingles flapped in the wind. The boys, one a slightly larger version of the other, ran around the corner into the backyard, the taller one holding a broken fence paling like a sword. They stopped and turned when they saw Wanda in the backyard.

"For the boys?"

"Yeah. For the boys."

"Nothing for you?"

"Of course, some for me."

"You don't be throwing no money around. What do you spend it on?" Vincent's voice was soft at the end of the question.

"You don't have to spend to be looking after yourself."

Vincent cleared his throat. "Can't hardly put that kind of money in the bank, though?"

Wanda paused. She pushed his arms away and reached into her back pocket for her cigarette package again.

"Well, no."

"So how do you keep your stash safe?"

"I got a safe spot. In the woodhouse."

She could hear the excitement rising up in Vincent's voice. "Where in the woodhouse?"

"Up in the beams." Her eyes scanned the yard, stopping on a five-gallon plastic bucket with a map of Newfoundland on the front of it. "In an old salt beef tub."

Vincent sighed and pulled her close. Wanda's shoulder crushed into his armpit, her face against his neck.

"You're some smart. Somewhere out in the open where no one would look to find it."

Wanda pulled her head back to look at him. "Yeah, that's me — sharp as a tack." She smiled and he laughed, squeezing her in closer. Fucker, she thought.

&roc;

JANICE SAW KATIE WAVING FROM the top of the hill. She was calling out to her but the wind was blowing the words away. Janice opened the gate and walked up the incline toward the house. The grass grew high on either side of the path. A vine of hops wound up an old pole that had once been a slight spruce tree, cut and peeled to make a fish flake and then lost to become driftwood. The wild snapdragons were small and buttery yellow.

Katie stood with a hand on her hip, a small spade in the other. She was smiling. "Come in. Come in the house and see Hector. He's doing well now." She turned, not waiting for an answer. Janice followed her into the house.

The windows were open and several cats were draped over the windowsills. From this location, they watched Katie as she gardened. Hector came out from behind the couch, bearing only a little weight on the front paw. He limped his way between Janice's feet, mewing greeting meows.

"I think he remembers you. He remembers that you helped him." Katie went into the pantry to put the kettle on the electric range. A book on the table was open and turned over onto the spread pages, its cracked spine facing upward. Janice looked at the dark painting on the front of the book, which seemed to consist mostly of snow and huddled figures.

Katie appeared at her elbow. "Do you like Dostoevsky? I actually prefer Tolstoy, I think. Of the Russians." Katie smiled, her face open, waiting for a response.

"I don't read," Janice said, taking her hand off the book. "I mean, I can read. I just don't read books."

Katie looked concerned. "Why not?"

Janice shrugged. "Just don't. Want some help with the tea?"

Katie ignored her offer. "How far did you get in school?"

"Grade eleven. I didn't write the final exams."

"Why?"

Janice looked out the window. "I started going out with Brendan that spring, so I spent most of the end of the school year at his place in St. John's. And then I had Bride."

"Brendan is her father, right?"

"He's dead," said Janice, not turning around.

Katie reached out and touched her shoulder. "I'm sorry. When did you lose him?"

Janice turned around. She had no expression on her face. "It was before Bride was born."

"Well, you did a good job of raising her on your own. She's got something special in her, I think."

"Well, not alone. There's Rupert."

"Oh, right. Rupert."

"Rupert loves her," Janice said, almost to herself. He does, she thought. I know he does.

"Your second husband?"

"I never married Brendan. That was before I was saved. I wasn't married then. When she was born."

"Saved? You mean in the Salvation Army?"

"Yes."

Katie did not seem impatient as she mentioned religion. She did not try to change the topic. She looked interested, not embarrassed.

"What made you join the Army?"

"It wasn't Brendan's dying, if that's what you're thinking. I just woke up one morning and I realized that I was wandering. No direction. I started going to church. I've felt better ever since." Until I looked at you, she thought.

"Does Bride go to church? Rupert?"

Janice sighed. "She's not the most obedient child."

Katie took her arm and motioned toward the couch. They sat. "How do you mean?"

"She won't come home when I tell her. And she certainly won't go to church. She goes around with that Wanda Stuckless to spite me, I think."

"Wanda's a bit rough, but she's not bad, Janice. She just hasn't had a lot of opportunities in the world, you know. Her parents can't give her much, and I don't just mean money."

"No. Well, Bride is young. She's so young. She don't know nothing yet."

"How old were you when she was born?"

"Seventeen."

"So a year younger than she is now?"

Janice pulled her feet up underneath her. "I didn't know nothing."

"But you learned. And Bride will learn."

"I don't want her to have to learn the way I did, with a small baby."

Katie began stroking her wrist, tracing the pattern that the sinews and veins made.

"Brendan used to do that too."

"What?"

"Stroke my wrist like that."

Katie let go. "I think the kettle is boiled." She got up and went into the pantry. Janice thought, why did I say that? Now she thinks I'm sad. And stupid.

Katie came back with a tray of cups and tea things. She put it between them on the couch.

"You know, you can finish your high school if you want to, Janice. You can do it by correspondence. You don't even have to go to classes."

Janice shook her head. "Too late now."

"You really think that people get too old to learn new things?"

Janice stopped her hand as she reached toward a plate of cookies. "Well, no."

"Then why don't you finish your high school?"

"What if I fail?"

"You won't fail. I'll help. I'm not going away this summer and I have nothing to do."

"Katie, that will be an awful lot of work for you."

Katie looked pleased. "No, it will be work for you. I will enjoy helping." She laughed. "What a wonderful project for the summer, Jan. We'll get you graduated."

Jan. No one has ever called me Jan, she thought.

∽○∽

THE SUN WAS GOING DOWN as Wanda scooped the salt beef bucket from behind the house. Someone had half-filled it with shells from the beach. She dumped them into the grass and walked into the woodhouse. Her brothers were trying to nail boards together, the hammer too big for their small hands. They looked up when her shadow fell across them.

"Why don't you make like hockey players and get the puck outta here?" she said with humour in her voice.

The boys sensed that she was in a good mood. "Can't you see we're busy?" said Corey.

Wanda reached down and clipped him on the side of the head. He winced.

"Go on now, fuck off like you're told."

They went out and Wanda shut the door behind them. Only a little light came in from a cracked window, the wood piled almost halfway up its height. With the door closed, the scent of spruce sap from the dry wood was almost overpowering. It felt like Christmas, except for the smell of cat shit, which wafted up from the sawdust on the floor.

Frig. I got to close up this door in the nights so that the cats aren't in here. She stood on the chopping block, reached her hand up into the rafters and waved it around, confirming the space. Then she stepped back down and pulled a wad of cash out of her pocket. She dropped five twenties into the tub and put the lid on.

That should do it for now, she thought.

～∞～

THEY SAT ON THE TAILGATE of Wayne's truck. The moon rising over the pond made the water metallic. The bulk of the party had gathered in a clearing at the edge of the pond, lying on the grass, leaning on beer cases.

Wanda had pulled Bride away. For a draw, she said. As Wanda licked the edge of the rolling paper to seal the joint, Bride thought about how young she looked. The moonlight made Wanda's face seem soft, and she almost reached out her hand to touch her prominent cheekbone. Wanda closed her eyes as she licked the glue edge of the paper, and Bride could see how Wanda would look if she were sleeping.

The flame broke the darkness open and blinded them both for a moment. Wanda handed the joint to Bride, exhaling and looking out into the pond. They were silent as they smoked. Bride lay back into the pan of the truck, her arms over her head, smiling up at the stars. She felt Wanda shift her ass back farther onto the tailgate and lie next to her. They stayed still, side by side, for what seemed a very long time.

Wanda spoke first. Her voice was croaky from the weed.

"You're some close to Wayne now."

"Close?"

Wanda cleared her throat. "Yeah. Close." She giggled a bit. "You two are together every night."

"Yeah." Bride smiled up at the sky, leaning her head against Wanda's shoulder. "Yeah, most nights."

"So?"

"So what?"

"So, do you love him?"

Bride started to giggle. "I don't know."

"You're not going to stay here with him, are you?"

Bride rocked her head to find the most comfortable part of Wanda's shoulder. "No. You know I'm not."

Wanda's frame shook as she coughed. Bride could feel the air being pushed out of her.

"Is he any good?"

Bride sighed.

"So he is?"

"Wanda, he's your cousin."

Wanda started to laugh, big belly laughs. Bride joined in. The truck shook. They stopped suddenly, both gasping for air.

"So is he?"

"Wanda, I don't want to talk about this."

"You think that because he's my cousin you can't tell me if he is a good lay?"

Bride rolled onto her side and raised her head up on her hand. "He's great, okay," she said, not smiling.

Wanda sat up, looking out onto the pond. Laughter echoed out over the water from the party. The girls were silent.

⌒o⌒

MYRA POURED HER TEA OUT into the saucer to cool. The cup, emptied of half of its contents, sat on the placemat next to the saucer of caramel-coloured tea, lightened and thickened with evaporated milk. The pine table was covered with a tablecloth of crocheted roses and a further layer of thick, soft plastic.

Myra sat at the table alone, staring at the cold tea, the tea that she made for drinking. Janice would not be home for hours. Something was bothering her. She could see it on her face as she spoke to Bride about staying out all night. She seemed to be going through the motions of the chastisement.

She turned to the stove to shut off the burner under the kettle and reached for a box of loose tea behind the tin where she kept her baking spices, the special tea that she used to read the cup.

She poured a little hot water onto the loose tea leaves. She stood and looked out the window again, making sure that Janice was not coming home. The tea leaves floated in a pool at the bottom. She flipped the cup over swiftly into her saucer. Her hand hovered above it for a moment, until she saw the amber liquid seep around the base of the inverted cup. She flipped it back. The leaves clung around the top of the cup. She had left too much liquid in it, maybe. It looked like a commotion. The leaves were all bunched up in knots. Conflict.

She took the cup from the table and rinsed it under the tap water, the leaves swirling down the drain.

∽∘∾

THE MEN STOOD ON THE WHARF, all of them looking out into the sound. Eugene turned to watch Janice on her way down the hill to the cove.

"There comes your in-law there, George."

The men turned. A few laughed. George stood on the wharf, his hands in his pockets. His rubber boots stuck out like pontoons. He was a thin man with lean limbs and an enormous belly.

"Wha?" He left his mouth open after he spoke.

Eugene smiled. "Well, I've been seeing Bride in the truck with Wayne most nights since he come home. I figure it won't be long now."

"Won't be long till wha?" His mouth stayed open again.

Eugene put his big hands out in front of him to make a belly swollen with baby. "You and Janice Marsh will be related sooner than you think if you don't get that boy away from her."

"Not much I can do to keep him from getting his tail. He's a man now. So long as she don't try to convert him over to the Army, I don't suppose it matters who he takes up with."

"Janice will be dragging you and the young fellow up to the mercy seat, trying to save your souls and get yous into the Salvation Army uniform if Wayne knocks her up." He smiled, a private smile, as if he were imagining George in a soldier's uniform. "Mark my words."

George turned around and looked at Janice as she stepped onto the wharf. "Take a lot more than a good lay to get me to convert and put the 'S's on my collar."

The men stopped laughing as Janice neared, her face unsmiling and preoccupied.

"George. I need to talk to you."

George spat, a long, low stream of mucus squirting over the head of the wharf. He did not turn to acknowledge her.

"Well, I'm right here." The other men smiled.

"I need to talk to you about the money you owe me. I didn't figure you wanted to stand here on the wharf and talk about that."

George spat again. He did not turn to look at her.

"You'll get your money, maid. The tourists is back now, down here trying to see whales and icebergs. I should have some money Friday. I expect you will get paid for the bit of food that we buys from you then."

Janice still did not move, but stood talking to the back of his head, as the other men looked at her.

She folded her arms. "So you'll pay me when you gets your tourist money, then?"

He turned now to look at her. "Don't sound like you approves of the way I makes my living. You sells them fellows a few cases of beer and a scattered pack a chips when they down here sightseeing."

"I never said nothing about where you gets your money. I just wants what's owed me."

George had turned to face the other men now.

"I deserves that mainland money, every Jesus cent of it. It's easier money than anything that I ever earned in my life, but I'd rather be out there catching fish than answering stunned questions — 'What is a jigger for, Captain Lambert?' Scraping irritating mainlanders up off the bottom, where you is going to end up if you don't stop leaning out over the side with that camera. Not like I didn't work bloody hard when we was at the fish. Just look at my hands. These are a workingman's hands. I got scars like Jesus had on his hands when they took him off the cross. The government nailed us all on the cross when they shut down the fishery." He looked into the faces of the other men, his face challenging one of the others to contradict him.

"That's blasphemy, George. You're hardly the Saviour. Jesus wouldn't say that about people. Them people don't mean no harm. They just don't know nothing."

"Well, Jesus wouldn't be going around debt collecting in public neither, would he? He gave to the poor instead of going around money-grubbing."

He continued to ignore Janice.

"It was the federal government that screwed-up the fishery and made sure that every Jesus cod in the North Atlantic was scooped-up by foreign trawlers. We told them that the quotas were too big, but they knew better than a bunch of uneducated fishermen, them scientists did. They should have to pay us for the way that crowd up in Ottawa —" he paused here and pointed his finger toward the land, "— for the way that crowd up in Ottawa snarled-up everything here."

Janice's mouth was pinched. "What the federal government did to you don't mean that you don't have to pay me what you owe me. I got to make a living, you know."

"You could do what other women do. Send your husband out to work."

"Rupert's not well. He's home today with a bad back."

George almost looked sorry for her as she spoke. "Janice, he's home every day with a bad back."

"He can't help it. He's sick."

He turned to look out over the wharf. "Maybe you'd better head home and say your prayers now, Janice. Pray for his recovery. Pray them mainlanders are buying plane tickets and them retarded rain outfits that costs more than my boat."

She turned and walked back toward the beach.

"Yeah, you better pray," Eugene added, "for your daughter."

The laughter drowned out the last comment. Janice walked up the hill from the wharf.

"Nice ass on her, you know," said Eugene.

"Yeah, but it's too full of the Holy Spirit to get anything else up there, my son," said George. He spat.

∽◦∾

KATIE LEANED OVER HER, DRAPING her arm around the back of her chair as Janice sat at the kitchen table.

"This part is pretty mechanical, but they might ask a multiple-choice, so you should know it." Her hand reached across and flipped through the pages of the chapter. "It's pretty short."

Katie was close, close enough for Janice to smell the shampoo that she used and the underlying scent of her hair. She breathed deeply, pulling the fragrance of her into her lungs, able to taste it in her mouth.

"Parts of speech. The only real way to do this is to understand the concept and then practice picking the parts out of a sentence. What is a noun?"

"A thing," said Janice, swallowing.

"Only a thing?" Katie's face was so close to her now that she could feel her breath on her skin.

"No, a person too." A sweet, wonderful person, she thought.

"Good. But what is it in relation to the rest of the sentence?"

Janice paused. "It's the thing," she wavered, "the thing or person that the action is about."

"Excellent," said Katie, smiling. She reached over to stroke Janice's cheek as if she were touching a child, rewarding her with intimacy for her success. She pulled her hand back as if it had been a casual touch, as if she had not moved her thumb ever so slightly along Janice's cheekbone.

"I'll get us a snack," she said, straightening her body.

Janice stared at the page. The words looked faraway, the parts no longer distinguishable from the whole.

∽∽

EUGENE WAS STANDING IN THE back of the truck, holding the moose head that rested on the cab with one hand, and waving a beer bottle with the other. The moose was at least twelve hundred pounds. The antlers were four, almost five feet across.

Eugene whooped. "Look at the size of this bugger, would you?" he called to Derek, who was running across the road, pulling his jacket on as he came.

"You should have been there Derek, boy. Raymond took him down with one shot, right through the rib cage. He tore the heart right out of the fucker. When we slit him open, the heart was all ripped up." He wiped the snot from his nose with the sleeve of his work shirt. He held his beer in the same hand and as he lifted his arm, some of the liquid poured out into the truck. "Give us a hand."

Raymond had turned off the engine and stepped out of the cab. Placing one foot on the back wheel, he swung himself into the pan of the truck next to his brother. Derek jumped over the tailgate and slipped in a pool of moose blood. They had quartered it up to get it out of the woods. The air smelled of wet fur, mud and raw meat.

"We're going to be having the biggest Jesus barbecue that you ever seen in your life, buddy," Eugene said. "Not until Jerry butchers it up into steaks, of course. But just wait till the weekend, my son. There'll be beer and moose as far as the eye can see — just like Jesus and the loaves and fishes. We'll invite everyone. Give us a hand now to get it into the woodhouse. Missus is going to be vicious with me about this if I brings a mess into the house, blood all over her clean kitchen floor. I'd rather face a pissed-off moose any day than the Missus when she's after seeing a big mess in the house. At least it's legal to shoot the moose — although not in July, mind you. But if I gives everyone a bit of moose, then no one can call the Forestry officers if they got illegal moose meat in the deep freeze."

Eugene opened the tailgate and the blood dripped from the metal.

∽∘∾

AS JANICE WALKED, SHE COULD hear the voices of the men — broad, flat and excited — and the sound of car doors and feet on gravel. As she rounded the turn, Raymond and Derek lifted a quarter of the animal. From where she stood she could see that their hands were wet, the sleeves of their shirts red-brown. The blood dripped from the gap where the tailgate hinged to the body of the truck. The men looked up. She nodded and kept walking.

If she had known what the commotion was about, she would have not turned her head. There was that big, fat jackass Eugene standing up in the pickup, waving his beer. And then there was Derek, sucking around trying to get a few steaks by helping them unload.

Eugene looked at her. "Hey, Janice."

She stopped. The head sat on top of the truck cab, the eyes half closed. When the head was removed — when there were no dead eyes staring at them — there was no guilt in breaking the limbs and spilling the hot guts out onto the ground. It had just become a carcass, not capable of sound or expression. From where she stood, she could smell the scent of something dead, male sweat and gasoline fumes from the truck engine mixing and rising on the evening breeze. She closed her throat against the smell and started to walk again.

"Come on over here this weekend, and we'll get you a big piece a meat, Janice maid," Eugene yelled after her.

∽∘∾

EUGENE SNORTED THROUGH HIS NOSE and lowered his voice. "I don't suppose she'll be wanting any meat, though. I think her and that mainlander schoolteacher is 'vegetarians,' if you take my meaning."

"Vegetarians? Them two?" said Derek

"Yes, my son. They've been up there in that house together half the summer, and I don't expect that they've been playing checkers."

"Lord Christ," said Derek, shaking his head. He pulled his shoulder up to wipe the sweat from his cheek. A rusty stain appeared on his face. "Sure this won't do at all."

"The vegetarianism?"

"Worse. I believes that that schoolteacher might be a Catholic. What is a good Army soldier like Janice doing with a Catholic girl?"

"Perhaps she's trying to teach her how to pray," said Raymond, as he struggled with a quarter of moose.

Eugene smiled. "I bet they spends all night on their knees."

The laughter was delighted, shocked, young-boy laughter in the deep, heavy voices of men.

"So, no meat at all for them, hey?" Eugene said.

"Nope. I hear they're pretty strict about it."

"Well, perhaps she'd change her mind when she got her lips wrapped around a piece."

They laughed again. Janice's figure turned the bend in the road on the way to the store.

ᗢ

IT WAS ALMOST DAWN WHEN Vincent opened the woodhouse door. The hinges squeaked loudly. He stopped, holding his breath so that he could hear any responding sound from inside the house. Nothing. He stepped inside.

The chopping block sat in the middle of the shed, the axe leaning off to the side of a stack of wood. Above it, Vincent could see the white shape of a tub that sat in the crossbeams. Shit, she's cocky. Right out in the open. He hopped up onto the chopping block and reached for the bucket.

Standing there in the new light he counted the money.

Five single bills. Cunt.

He dropped them back into the tub, snapping the lid down with the heel of his hand.

Tricky, fucking cunt.

༄༅

WANDA COULD HEAR A SOUND from outside, close by. Then another, but maybe from inside this time. Then another. The boys were in the kitchen. Wanda turned over and opened her eyes. The faded purple flowers on the wallpaper came into focus slowly. Her mind had not fully awakened and she did not recognize the patterns as roses. The swirls and segments of the petals took on the shape of a girl's head and neck, the face turned away. She adjusted her perspective and the shape went back to the cupped bowl of a rose, with wisps of leaves at its base. Through the wall, she could hear Ivey snoring. Her medication usually kept her in bed until mid-afternoon. Just before the boys came back from school, she would rouse herself in search of another pill.

Lynfield would have left at dawn, letting the sound of his footsteps tell him when he had ventured off the stone path onto the soft grass. Men get to walk away because they have a reason, Wanda thought. Ivey can't go away like Dad, so she leaves in her mind.

Downstairs came a thud, the sound of something heavy, like the body of a boy falling. A few minutes later, her door opened.

Her brother stood there silently at first, and then he spoke her name.

"What?" she said, not turning over.

"Corey fell off the chair trying to reach the Coco Puffs."

Wanda's head lifted off the pillow. "I'll be down in a minute. Don't go climbing no more. I'll get the breakfast."

The door fell closed. Wanda rolled over and pulled herself up. Her nipples were tender against the flannel of her pyjamas.

Fuck, she thought, now I'm going to get my period, too. I'll be puffy for days.

Her feet were cold on the linoleum as she walked down the hall toward the bathroom.

꿍

WANDA LAY NEXT TO VINCENT in the grass, the outline of their bodies pressed into the greenness. He lay with an arm under his head, folded back so that his hand was tucked under his shoulder blade. The other hand rested on Wanda's thigh, the worn cotton of her jeans thin and soft. He could feel the small muscles in her skinny leg flex slightly as she shifted to finish buttoning her shirt. She tucked herself in close to him and sighed. For a thin woman, she always seemed extraordinarily warm, her skin hot against his own. He always imagined that skinny women would feel cold. Fat people looked so warm all the time, but the skinny seemed too insubstantial to retain any heat.

She stroked his stomach, running her fingers along the swatch of flesh between his navel and the waistband of his jeans. Vincent thought about how much he enjoyed the light tracking of the pads of her fingers through the hair on his stomach, how much he had enjoyed spending this last month with her. Too bad, he thought. Too bad I'm going to have to leave her behind.

She stopped stroking him. "This fucking place. Waiting for things to happen — that's all that people do here. Wait until spring, then the ice will be gone out of the sound."

It surprised him that she had been thinking too, as if lying warm beside him was not enough for her.

"Or wait until the election, and then there might be pavement. Wait until there's an oil well, and then there might be jobs. It's like no one can get up on their hind legs and get anything on their own."

He had stopped thinking about her body now. "What do you mean?"

"This is a place where nothing happens. That's because real life is going on somewhere else, where people are doing things. People here are all waiting. The old are waiting to die. The young are waiting to grow up and leave. The religious for Jesus, and the fishermen for the cod to come back."

The words poured out and she stopped to inhale.

"When me and Bride get our cash sorted out, I'm going to stop waiting. We'll go somewhere where people don't wait for someone else to make their lives happen."

"Where you going?" he said, although what he thought was, what money?

She pulled her arm back, as if she had said too much, and wanted to take it all back, the words, the touch.

"Toronto. Maybe."

"Why Toronto?"

"Because it's not here."

She sat up and shook the dry grass out of her hair. "I gotta go now," she said, and stood without kissing him goodbye.

Vincent watched Wanda as she walked out over the hill toward the community. As she walked further away, the peculiarity of her movements became more pronounced. She hurried, stepping quickly with long strides. She swung her arms to counterbalance the movement in her lower body. She's a little windmill of a woman, he thought. Thin propellers whirling in the wind. She bent into her motion, her head forward, making her hair swing like a curtain in the breeze. The movements of limb, torso, head and hair were all slightly uncoordinated from one another. Vincent was reminded of a mechanical object in motion, jolting forward.

He decided to let her fall almost out of sight before he followed. The sun was close to setting and he would lose the light fast. He saw a flash of red as she jumped the fence next to Tavener's barn. Her head and shoulders fell out of sight around the corner of the building. He stood and prepared to follow.

It was hard to keep up with her, not because she moved fast, but because she could edge her thin body into spaces that he was not close enough to see — between woodsheds, through the rungs of ranch-style fences, the space between a garage and a pickup. Then she stepped into the road and his view of her was clear, unobstructed, a good shot for a sniper.

A hedge of rose bushes blocked his view of her as she left the main road and walked up the gravel driveway to her house. He stood in the lee of them and listened to the rocks crunching under her feet, looking for a way to follow her without being seen. On the left, a fence separated the Stuckless property from the lower yard of the Taveners'. On the right was the beginning of a rocky hill that descended toward the beach. He stood on tiptoes, raising his head over the roses, the dark pink flowers silky against his cheek.

She vanished around the corner of the house, into the grass where he could no longer hear her footsteps. Behind the house, the woods were dark and ran up the hill in a gradual incline. The density and the height made a perfect vantage point for viewing the back of the Stuckless house.

No more following, he thought. Next time I'll wait for her to come to me.

∽◦∾

THAT WOMAN. GIRL-WOMAN, WHATEVER she was. Lord Jesus. Wayne squinted his eyes against the reflection of the sun in the water. He sat on the wharf, elbows on his knees. At ten in the morning, the sun had grown strong, but not enough to counteract the wind. Blowing in off the water from the northeast, it brought the chill of the Labrador Current onto the land.

The Current flowed south from the Arctic, delivering huge icebergs that floated in its arms, waltzing and spinning down along the headlands. The Gulf Stream met the Current off the Grand Banks. The clash of the currents — one a stream of frigid water, travelling in icy armour, the other tropical and subtle — impounded the whole of the Banks in fog.

Stray pieces splintered off the icebergs and drifted into the bays and inlets. When Wayne was a child, he stood on the deck of his father's boat and felt the cold envelop him as a berg passed. It sweat a vapour that froze his breath in his mouth, casting a shadow over the longliner, blocking off the sun as it floated by. Its milky-green whiteness shone from underneath the black water, and Wayne could see that the base of the berg was vast. George kept them as faraway from it as possible without bottoming the longliner on the shoals. If the iceberg drifted into the shallows, its big bottom would stick firmly in the sand and slowly be killed by the sun. It would be caught by forces more stealthy and subtle than those its own brute mass could employ.

The wind blew over the water at such a speed that the sun had no opportunity to warm it. It took the cold from the water and spread it over the land. The clouds it pushed seemed like icebergs that had been freed from their mortal weight, ephemeral and soft in the sky.

The waves were diamond-studded in the morning sun. Peaks in the wave patterns became prisms that filter the sunlight, separating it into its base colours. Water breaks all matter down into its primal parts. The spruce that falls from the cliff sheds its bark, which peels and washes away — a snake's old skin — the salt leaches out the sap and softens the wood, the limbs come off, weakened at the joints by the action of the waves and the resoluteness of the rock. When the skeleton washes up on the beach, all that remains is the grey-silver driftwood.

As the wind pushed the water into swells and dips, Wayne recognized that the water had a female form. The small rolling waves that had begun as powerhouses deep in the bay were now tiny rounded lengths of water, like the firm muscles of a girl's leg. The flat pools that lay between the rocks were the stomach muscles, hard beneath a subtle layer of fat. Everywhere he looked, he could see her body, as if Bride were trying to take shape in the waves.

I'm not a well man he thought, touching his stomach through his T-shirt. The acid rose in his throat, he turned his head and spat out the bitter saliva. It hit the water, plopping like a small stone. Spit becomes salt water. Everything comes back to the sea in the end. Rain, spit, ice, love — the sea is the only thing big enough to swallow it all.

He could hear George's voice now, calling him from the long-liner. "Time to get the stuff on board." His father waved at him, holding something in his hand. As he got closer, he could see that it was the thermos.

"Guess you're going to need this today. Out gallivanting around all night. You're going to pay for that. Who was you with?"

"Bunch from down the cove. Paul, Wanda, Nancy." He paused. "Bride."

George snorted. "Bride? Bride Marsh? Oh, you better be careful of that one, or she'll be trying to save your soul. You'll have to promise yourself to the Lord before you gets anything off of her."

"She's not like her mother. And besides, I'm not going out with her."

"Nice, though. You should be. If I was you, I'd be right after her. But you wouldn't get your skin in a barrel of pussy."

"Jesus, Father. You shouldn't be saying them things. You're too old to be thinking about girls that way."

"Too old? My son, if you don't want me to pitch you arse over kettle over the wharf, then I wouldn't be saying nothing about me being too old. Your old feller don't drop off after you turns fifty, you know."

Wayne stood still as George turned toward the cabin.

"Don't say nothing about Bride again."

George looked back at his son. Wayne could feel that his fists were bunched up beneath the cuffs of his jean jacket. The tendons of his neck were tight. The smirk went out of George's eyes.

"Well, come on then, we got to get them mainlanders out for their tour." The sarcasm had come back into his voice. "Hope you got your guitar on board, 'cause you know how they likes to see us doing jigs and singing "Lukey's Boat." We got a regional stereotype to perpetuate today."

His speech was interrupted by the sound of a car taking the turn at the top of the hill too fast. Gravel sprayed into the guardrail, making a hiss and ping.

"Fucking mainlanders," said George.

∽o∽

BLACK AS COAL DUST. NO stars. The clouds hung heavy in the sky that evening and blocked out all points of light. Wanda stood on the chopping block. As she put her hand into the blackness of the rafters, a piece of wood that Lynfield had stacked there fell, knocking some plastic tubing to the ground. A cat shot out from under a woodpile, its feet making soft frantic sounds on the sawdust floor.

Wanda stood with her arm in the air, still and quiet. Her blood was hot and fast. A fist clenched her heart.

A cat. A frigging cat. She lifted her arm again and the smooth side of the plastic tub touched her palm. Reaching up her other arm, she took it down.

The five bills were inside. She rubbed them between her thumb and forefinger thinking, does this feel like money? The paper was worn soft. She held each bill to her nose in the darkness and inhaled.

The smell of money — earthy with a faint tinge of something acidic, almost vinegary.

Yes, she thought, this is money. Real money. But what exactly is this cocksucker about?

∽o∽

WAYNE SAT IN THE TRUCK outside Bride's house. Inside, he could see Janice and Myra moving about the kitchen, dishes in their hands. He had seen Bride get up from the table and walk out of the room. The women looked at him waiting in the truck but didn't wave or nod.

Bride had come back into the kitchen and stopped. Myra said something. Bride put her hands on her hips, raising her shoulders.

Great, he thought, now she'll be in a bitter mood. Janice was standing at the stove with her back to the room. She turned around, a pot in her hand, to speak to the other women. He saw Bride walk across the kitchen quickly, disappearing from view until she walked around the corner of the house.

She slammed the door of the truck. Her jaw was tense. She looked at him and said, "What's going on tonight?"

Wayne shrugged. "Some of the boys are in on the nut garden drinking."

"Well, let's go then," she said. "You got beer, right?"

He put the truck in drive and pulled away. "Yeah," he said. "Something wrong?"

She had pulled down the sun visor and was running the tip of her index finger around the perimeter of her lips. Wayne adjusted his position in the seat.

"Mom and Nan are giving me a hard time about you."

"What about?"

"You're too old for me."

He took one hand off the wheel as he drove and reached over to stroke her knee.

"Do you think so?"

She turned her head, considering the question.

"No," she said. "I think I'm more grown-up than you, even though you're seven years older than me."

He laughed even though she was not trying to be funny.

"You're always flattering me," he said, stroking her leg now. "That's why you're so easy to love."

Wayne looked at her, taking his eyes off the road for a moment, just slightly turning his head.

"Yeah, that's what they all say — I'm easy to love."

"Well, you are," he said, his voice serious this time.

"Let's just go drinking," she said, pulling down the sun visor to look in the mirror again.

❧

VINCENT WAS WALKING ON THE woods road toward the nut garden. He could tell from the cars parked by the side of the road that it was going to be a big party. People from all over the island, not just the harbour. Long weekend, he thought. Wanda will be here. A buck to be made tonight, for sure. And she'll have to take her cash home.

The cars were parked on the edge where the road sloped into the trees, tilted toward the woods. Wayne and Bride were here. Maybe Wanda came with them. He noticed the keys dangling in Wayne's ignition.

Stunned, fucking bayman, he thought. That man won't see it coming. And he won't see what that Bride will do to him either. He thinks he got it all under control, but she got him driving her around and doing whatever she tells him. He's going to be some surprised when she's gone and he's left here holding his dick in his hand. Then he's just going to be another unemployed asshole looking for a woman.

Not me, thought Vincent. I got a plan. Wanda's a part of it, for sure. But it don't depend on her agreeing to nothing.

❧

THE TRUCKS WERE ALL PARKED along the side of the narrow woods road that ran behind the school. Wayne could hear the boys laughing in the garden. They were sitting close to the brook, the beer cooling in the small stream that flowed out of Beaver Pond and wound across the meadow. A little sun remained, although it was sinking. Some of the girls stood smoking. He could feel their focus shift to him and Bride as they walked toward the crowd on the meadow. Bride carried a dozen Black Horse under her right arm. She pushed his hand away when he tried to take it from her. Wayne held her other hand, sticky with the heat of their bodies.

"Make the missus carry the beer there Wayne," said Derek. "Good man. Get her trained early. Nothing like a strong young maid." He licked his lips as he smiled at Bride, his eyes lingering on the shape of her breasts under her T-shirt.

Bride put the beer down and pulled open the case. "Don't make me come over there and beat the face off you tonight, Derek."

"Sure I never said nothing. I just said you was a strong young maid, nothing wrong with that. That's what every man wants in his bed."

Bride sat on the beer case. "I don't think you're going to get to be too choosy about what kind of woman you gets in your bed. I think they only sells one kind of the inflatable ones."

Derek's mouth was smiling, but his eyes were hard. He looked away from Bride to Wayne. "She's got a mouth on her. You'd do best to keep it fulled up, if you know what I mean."

The laughter of the boys made Wayne's scalp prickle with heat.

"Shut your face before I beats it off. Come on, Bride," Wayne said. He pulled her up from the beer case. "I think we'd better have a walk." He paused. "Don't want to have to watch you hurt Derek."

She had taken his hand without hesitation, no questions. She is starting to trust me, he thought. They turned to walk down toward the pond. Wayne could hear the other boys continue the conversation that they stepped out of.

"Some ass on her," said Colin.

Derek took a long pull on his beer. "Yeah, but she got attitude problems."

∽∘∾

THEY WERE SITTING ON THE bank of Beaver Pond. Wayne was behind her as she leaned back into him, her legs pulled up against her chest, her feet crossed at the ankles, his arms wrapped around her.

"I need to know something," Bride said.

She could feel him hesitate. "Anything," he said.

"Do you think like they do?"

"Derek, you mean?"

"Yeah. Do you think of me as a piece of meat?"

Wayne sighed. "Derek's not very bright," he said. "Derek's more interested in trying to get the better of you than in being close to you." He squeezed her as he said this. "He wants you to think he's the big man."

Bride turned her head so that she was looking up at Wayne. "But I don't think that. I think he's a giant arsehole. He don't make me feel small, he just fucks me right off."

Wayne laughed. "That's what I mean. Not very smart."

Bride leaned her head back against his collarbone.

"You never answered my question."

"What question?"

"How do you think of me?"

"I think you're the most wonderful girl in the world."

"Because I've got big tits?"

"No," he sighed. "Not because you got big tits. Cheryl Martin's got bigger tits than you and I don't go out with her."

They both laughed.

"Come away with me next weekend, Bride."

She pushed her back into his chest, wiggling her shoulders.

"Maybe," she said. "I'll see."

∞∾

BRIDE WALKED OVER TO WANDA, who was sitting with her back to Vincent. He stood, staring at her, smoking. Wayne went back to the truck for his cigarettes when they came up from the pond.

"We drove by your place tonight. Your father said you'd already left." She handed Wanda a beer from the case of Black Horse. "Here, have a dark pony."

Wanda sniffed and nodded as she took the beer from Bride. "Yeah, I had to meet my supplier."

Bride sat on the grass next to her. "Levi?"

"Shut up. He thinks no one knows he's the biggest supplier in this arm of the bay."

"Sorry. You okay?"

"Nah, I think I'm PMSing or something. My tits ache."

"Yeah, well, at least there's not a lot to hurt."

Wanda snorted. "What a bitch you are. Some friend."

They both laughed.

"It's the end of July. I know we said September, but I've been thinking that I might have enough in a few weeks, after I sell this lot. Ask your grandmother if you can have that money she's been promising."

"You want to go in a few weeks?"

Wanda sighed. "Bride I just can't take this bullshit anymore, you know? The boys are old enough now. I'll send them money from Toronto. You'll have to call your aunt too, see if we can stay with her for a while. And you'll have to tell your mother."

Bride looked away. "Yeah. I'll have to." She turned to watch Wayne walk back from the truck. He's beautiful, she thought. Shit, he's just frigging perfect. Now is the time. Time to make a move.

"Okay," she said to Wanda. "I'll ask."

"She's going to have a hairy conniption, you going away."

"You know, I don't think she was always like this. I think she was okay one time."

"You mean before you were born?"

"Yeah, before me. I saw this picture of them once, the two of them together, and she looked almost normal."

Like a normal woman, she thought. He looked already dead. They were standing, arms around each other's waists, a truck parked behind them, water in the background. She was probably pregnant by then. The photo was in a velvet-covered jewellery box with an old rhinestone necklace.

She spoke again. "You know how sometimes you look at someone and you can see what they are going to look like when they're old?"

Wanda shrugged.

"They're the ones that people say, after twenty years she hasn't changed a bit. It's because the oldness was in them from the time they were kids. Well, there are some people you look at and you can see what they're going to look like dead. Maybe their death is in them from the beginning too."

"Bride, man. Sometimes you're real fucked up." Wanda shook her head slowly, not taking her eyes off her friend.

"My father, in the picture, he had this long, angular jaw." Bride stroked her own jaw to emphasize this. "He didn't look nothing like Roop. When I looked at him, I could imagine his mouth open, salt water spilling out of him on the autopsy table. I could see his eyes, staring up at the morgue ceiling, looking surprised."

"Now you're just being gross." Wanda turned her head like she was not listening anymore.

"His hair was red. I wondered if the colour of his hair would have seemed showy on a corpse," she paused for a second. "I'm glad I didn't get his red hair."

"Jesus, this is your father you're talking about."

Bride ignored her. "There's something sad about a flashy corpse. Those prom girls — the ones that die drunk in car accidents — must look so foolish lying there dead, bleeding in their taffeta dresses. That's what I always think the dead will look like — surprised or embarrassed."

She paused, thinking quietly for a moment. "But Mom, she looks so happy in the picture. She's leaning into him, and he's pulling her close, slightly off-balance. They were looking straight ahead, straight at the camera. 'This was us the summer before Bride was born.' That's what they would have said if they looked at the picture."

"You got way too much imagination. It's making you weird, Bride. I hope you don't talk to Wayne about stuff like this."

She interrupted her story. "Wayne? Of course not. He's a guy. He doesn't actually listen to me. But it's funny, you know," she said, switching back to the photo. "I could look at his face and see that my father was already dead. But looking at Mom's face, I couldn't see the way she is now."

"Maybe, back then, she couldn't see the way things would turn out either," said Wanda.

∽○∾

JANICE STOOD BY THE SINK, her left hip leaning into the cupboard. She held a mug in her right hand, the heat from the liquid blurring the air above it. Her eyes were focused somewhere outside the window, on the hills that surrounded the cove. Her shoulders rose as she inhaled suddenly, jolting her rib cage as if she were forgetting to breathe. Janice's lips turned up softly at the corners. She turned from the window to find herself in her mother's kitchen.

"Janice Marsh, you might as well tell me now."

"What are you saying?"

"You know full well what I'm saying. I want to know what is going on with you."

"Nothing. What are you getting on about?"

Myra lowered her voice, speaking more softly. "You know better than to lie to me, Janice. You haven't been yourself these last few weeks. So now you're going to tell me."

"Tell you what?"

"His name. You say you've been up to Katie's almost every night for weeks. I want to know who you've been meeting up with."

"There's no one. My word, Mom. I'm married." Dear blessed Jesus, Janice thought, she can divine things without even looking into the cup. She can look right through me. Janice was giddy as she left the kitchen. She willed her feet to walk firmly, but in spite of herself, she could feel the skip, the bounce in the balls of her feet.

When Janice opened the door to the bedroom, Bride was still sleeping. She was lying on the top of the blankets, her T-shirt beside the bed, her jeans and sneakers still on. She lay on her stomach, arms flung out like a hit-and-run victim. She woke when Janice sat on the bed, and pulled up a bra strap that had slid down her arm.

"Bride. Wake up. I'm going to work soon and I need you to get up and help Nan with the wash today. Come on, Bride. Up."

Bride rolled onto her back. Mascara smudges under both her eyes made her look even younger somehow. Her hair spilled across the pillow, dark against the perfect white of Myra's bleached pillowcase.

"Yeah, I'm up," she said swallowing, but not opening her eyes.

"Don't go back to sleep. Come on, get up."

"Jesus, Mother, give me a break, will ya? I was out late." She rolled over to face the wall, her eyes closed. Janice placed a hand on her shoulder.

"Where were you last night?"

"Out with the boys."

"Wayne?"

"Yeah, Wayne. And Paul, Wanda and Nancy."

"We talked about this. He's too old for you Bride. And no prize. Hanging around here with no job."

"He's just someone I hang around with," she said, turning over to face the wall again.

Janice got up to leave. "Well, you just be careful. And don't sleep all day."

She shut the door and walked back down the hallway to her own room. Who am I to tell her to be careful, she thought. Who am I to tell her anything at all?

∽∾

KATIE WAS ON THE OTHER side of the table reading, her brows pulled together in concentration. Janice looked down on the page in front of her, but her focus was on Katie's arm, resting on the table. It distracted her writing.

Katie looked up, pushing up her glasses. "Janice, I'm going to ask you something and you've got to keep it between you and me."

Janice felt her stomach contract. She nodded.

"Do you smoke weed?"

"Weed?" Janice felt her eyebrows rise up toward her hairline. Drugs. Oh Lord, she thought watching the look on Katie's face. Now she thinks I'm a prude.

"Marijuana." Katie looked down. "Never mind, just forget I asked you that, okay?"

"I haven't for a long time. Not since I started going to church."

"Oh," said Katie. "Right, sorry."

"Do you?"

"Sometimes."

Janice looked down at her textbook again and cleared her throat. "You got any?"

"Yes. But this is against your religion, right?"

Absolutely, thought Janice, this is absolutely wrong. "Yes. Well, no. No intoxicating liquor. But this is not really liquor."

"Not liquor."

"Well, maybe I could try it again."

"I feel like I'm pressuring you into this." Katie smiled. "But maybe we're too old for peer pressure, eh?"

Janice smiled. "Maybe not." How Canadian she sounds, thought Janice. Who says 'eh' except people on TV?

"We'll go out to the greenhouse," Katie said. "That way the whole harbour won't know we're smoking up."

∾∘∾

JANICE FELT THE SMOKE FILL her lungs. She exhaled slowly when she could hold her breath no more. She became aware of the knot of muscles between her neck and shoulder — hard, tense and with the consistency of cold rubber. The nerve that ran somewhere through the pelvis to the back of her legs vibrated as she shifted, and she imagined it stretched like a thick rubber band. Her hands were awful. They were twice as big as normal. Every heartbeat poured the blood into them, making them hot and swollen. She thought, if I touched her now, all I would feel is my own hands. It would be like holding her with the bandaged hands of a burn patient.

"We'll have a little nightcap," Katie had said. She's flirting with me now, Janice thought. They went outside, Katie leading the way to the greenhouse. She produced a perfectly rolled joint from inside her coat. She put it all in her mouth to wet it, lit it expertly and took small, quick puffs, her eyes squinting against the smoke. She handed it over. Janice felt the hard edges of the smoke cut her lungs. She tried to hold her breath but quickly began to cough. Katie laughed, giggling each time Janice tried to inhale.

Katie crossed her legs and bent forward, her body shaking with laughter, her blond curls falling down so that Janice could see the slender length of her neck. Janice laughed too. Looking at the white perfectness of the nape of Katie's neck made her realize that it was not safe to speak, so she let the laughter fall out of her mouth, loud and echoing in the small space.

Katie stopped, inhaling deeply, one hand held to her chest. "You know Jan, I was thinking that I might head up to the mainland for a while at the end of the summer."

"I could look after your cats while you're gone."

"Why don't you come with me instead? That way I could keep helping you with your course."

"I have the store. There's Mom and Bride. And Rupert."

"They'll be fine." Katie leaned forward and touched Janice's hand.

"I don't know. I have never been away before."

"Well, that's why you should come, see more of the country, come down to my brother's place by London. We can go into Toronto. Go up the Bruce Peninsula. It would be great."

Janice looked at her shoes. She felt less giggly now, more like the world had slowed down. "I don't know. I would have to think about it."

The moon was powerful and clear, gilding the yard with silver as if all the houses and each blade of grass had been coated in metal. Clouds hovered at the edge of the bright patch that the moon had made in the sky.

The greenhouse was bubble shaped. Katie had found that the

only way to grow anything on this island was to build a barrier to the wind and cold. Green shoots, ghostly in the moonlight, were pushing up out of the soil, protected from the winds by the glass. The women stood in the dirt track between the rows of new plants. A shadowy rake leaned against the glass with an old work shirt hanging from the handle. Buckets hung around the entrance, tipped at odd angles on the uneven ground. Katie's face was mostly shadows. The smell of damp earth mixed with the smoke, and for an instant Janice could see the garden that would bloom here by September — lush, the growth almost tropical on the barrens, protected by only a few panes of glass.

"I want you to come with me, Jan. It would be a great road trip. It could be so much fun." Katie took the joint back from Janice.

"So?" She paused only for a moment, expecting an answer. "Jesus, you're even more quiet when you're stoned. It usually turns most people into motormouths. What are you thinking in there, Jan?" Katie pointed at Janice's heart, not her head.

Janice felt her hands begin to throb again. They were leaden, too heavy to lift. She willed her tongue not to move and swallowed quickly.

"Jan? Why won't you go with me? Everything will be fine here while you're gone."

The words came out before she could stop them, her tongue releasing the thought before her brain could intervene. "I'm not worried about here."

"What do you have to worry about being on the road?"

"I'll be with you all the time."

"Do you mean you don't want to spend all that time with me?" Katie's brow pulled tight now, her eyes vulnerable.

Her face was tender and full of doubt. Janice leaned forward and kissed her, barely touching Katie's lips with her own. Katie pulled back slightly, and then returned the kiss.

"I'm sorry," said Janice, pulling away. "I'm real sorry." She opened the door of the greenhouse and walked quickly toward the garden gate.

∞∞

JANICE DID NOT GO BACK for her tutorial on Tuesday. She stood looking out the front window at Katie's house, the flowers in the window boxes, the curtains blowing in the wind. Janice could make out the dark shape of a cat pressed against a window screen. Katie would be in the kitchen, cutting and arranging food on plates. She would have taken out Janice's books and stacked them on the table. There would be an air of expectation in the house, the electricity of waiting for someone to arrive, the anticipation of a knock on the door.

Or maybe not. Maybe she doesn't want to see me today, Janice thought. How can I go back there after what I did? I'll just wait, she thought. I'll just wait and see.

She let the curtain drop back into place and went into the living room to turn on the television. The sound of people talking earnestly into a void filled up the room.

∞∞

DEREK SAT ON THE STACKED boxes of Carnation milk next to the counter. A few of the younger men, almost boys, stood around him, drinking pop from bottles, their Adam's apples bobbing with each swallow, long fingers loose around the clear glass. Uncle Heber, mostly deaf now, leaned over the counter reading last weekend's *Evening Telegram*.

Derek took a deep breath and pulled his spine up straight. His hands, with spread fingers, rested on each knee.

"You boys getting any?"

There was soft laughter, shuffling of feet on linoleum and finally a muffled, "Yeah." The friends of the young man who spoke turned to him laughing, striking him lightly with their elbows.

"I bet you're not getting nothing off that new school teacher that come here from the mainland, Matthew." Derek said.

"Her? Why would I want to? She's one weird missus. Got her head in the clouds, thinking about Shakespeare all the time."

"Her head's not always in the clouds. Sometimes it's between Janice Marsh's legs."

"Not true," said a boy with just the barest hint of blond on his upper lip.

The boys leaned forward now, the apathy and coolness gone out of their collective stance. No one lifted the pop bottles.

"What are you saying Derek?" said Matthew.

Derek smiled a small, pleased smile. He flexed his fingers, raising them up off his knee for a moment. "That's her woman," he said.

"Janice? Bride's mother? Sure Janice is not a dyke. She's a mother." A murmur of agreement came from the boys that stood around Matthew.

"And that Bride is a nice piece too," the younger boy with the ambitious moustache said quickly. They all laughed.

Derek reached up to his face and rubbed his cheekbones, his hand covering his smile. "Well, maybe a leopard can change her spots, as they say. Janice Marsh and that teacher are as close as two women can be." Derek's mouth was firm now, his chin tilted up in confidence.

"How would you know? They sell you a ticket?" said Matthew.

Derek spoke over the laughter. "Eugene saw them. Legs around each others heads, going right at it."

Matthew had no response to this, and the boys were distracted by the image in their minds.

Eugene, with Raymond in tow, opened the door to the small convenience store. Both men wore heavy plaid shirts, dusted with sawdust.

"Well now, speak of the devil," said Matthew.

"Which one of we devils was yous speaking about?" asked Eugene. Raymond was silent as he closed the door behind them.

Derek's shoulders lost the squareness that had been there before the door opened. "So you got your moose? When's that barbecue?"

Eugene opened his mouth to speak. Matthew said quickly, before he could answer, "We hear you been looking at a lot more than moose behinds lately."

Eugene's eyebrows shot up, his smile making the crow's feet at the corners of his eyes deepen and his face open. "Just what do you think I've been looking at, my son?"

"Derek says that you caught Janice Marsh and that school teacher doing the nasty."

"Blessed fuck, what have you been saying?" Eugene turned his whole body to face Derek, who shifted his weight so that he sat on the edge of the boxes. "I never told you no such thing." Eugene raised his hand now, pointing his thick finger at Derek.

"But you said so yourself that them two was queer."

"I might have said it, but I never told you I seen them at it."

The boys were all quiet now, eyes sliding back and forth from Eugene to Derek.

Derek sniffed, not meeting anyone's eyes. "I thought you saw them together. How else would you know?"

Eugene stood now in front of the counter. His twenty-dollar bill lay on Heber's newspaper. The old man looked up for the first time since the brothers entered the store and turned wordlessly to the shelf behind him. He pulled a green packet of Export A's from the shelf and opened the till to make change.

"Derek, you don't have to see a horse eat hay to know that he likely did so — especially if he spends a lot of time locked up in a barn full of it."

The boys hooted. Derek's lips quivered as if he were trying not to smile. Eugene retrieved his cigarettes and change from the counter. He turned and stepped through the door and Raymond followed. The bell above the door jingled and softened the loud laughter that he had left in his wake.

"Poor ole Rupert," Derek said. "Losing her. To a woman."

∽o∾

HE SAID "PLEASE" WITH SO much want in his voice that Bride could feel "yes" taking shape in her mouth. She shook her head. I want to go down the sound with him, she thought. It's not that I don't trust him, I just don't trust myself. Why is it that girls are always trying to figure out if we are trading sex for affection, or sex for lies? I look at him sometimes, I can smell him, and I want to touch my lips to his skin. That's all I want — skin against skin.

But I look around me and I see what skin on skin leads to. Look at Wanda. She thinks she's fucking Vincey, but he's fucking her.

"I don't think that Mom would be cool with me and you going away by ourselves. I could do it if there were a whole bunch of us."

His shoulders dropped. He put his hands back on the wheel. "Yeah," he sighed. "Yeah, I guess that's just not going to work."

They sat in silence. She slid over to him, lifting his arm around her shoulders, tucking herself in next to him, turned her face upward and kissed him, her tongue in his mouth, teasing his, pulling it into her own mouth. The whiskers of his moustache were rough against her lips, making them sore. He held her cheek in his hand, his thumb under her chin. She could feel her pulse beat against his fingers. Her hands were on his chest, stroking him.

He broke off the kiss and put his lips to her ear.

"This weekend," he said. "I want you to come with me this weekend."

"Yes."

✎

WANDA WAS FOLDING LAUNDRY. A small grey tabby had settled into the hot clothes and was being rearranged as she sorted.

Bride sat in a chair to the side of the television. Lynfield sat on the other side, his face held close to the screen.

"What's that Peter Mansbridge talking about? Where did that bomb blow up?" Lynfield watched the news every evening. Wanda always made fun of him. "Might as well be a big radio for all Dad knows. He thinks Peter Mansbridge still has hair. And he thinks Ian Hanomansing is Scottish."

Bride motioned her head toward the kitchen. Ivey sat at the kitchen table, picking lint off socks. Wanda stacked another pile in front of her.

"Here Ivey, knock yourself out."

Bride pulled Wanda by the arm into the corner of the kitchen. Ivey paid no attention to them.

"I need you to do something for me," Bride said.

"What?"

"This weekend I'm with you, okay? Don't go walking by the house without me. We're going camping down the sound."

Wanda sneered. "You're going with him, aren't you?"

"Okay, yeah, but Mom don't need to know, so I'm gone with you and some other people from Lower Side Harbour. All you got to do is keep out of Mom's way, is all."

"Sure, I can do that," said Wanda. "No problem. I'll cover for you."

She lowered her voice more. "Did you talk to your grandmother about the money yet?"

"Not since a while ago, but it won't be a problem. I'll talk to her after the weekend."

"Do it soon," said Wanda. Her eyes slid over to Ivey, who stared straight ahead, her hands moving slowly over a sock. "I'm almost ready," she said. "Soon. And your mom too." She put her hand on Bride's upper arm and squeezed. "I have to go, Bride."

"Yeah," said Bride, pulling free. "I'll talk to her."

∽○∾

"NAN?" BRIDE SAT DOWN ON the couch where Myra was knitting, trying to make use of the last light that came in the front window of the house.

"What, my duckie?" She put down the needles.

"You know how we talked about me going away?"

"Up to Cecilia's?"

"Yes. Well, now that school is over I think we're ready, me and Wanda. I think we should be getting things ready to go."

Her grandmother smiled. "You talk to your mother?"

"Not yet."

"Well, you got to talk it over with her, Bride. She won't like it, but she'll get used to it. It'll take time, is all."

Bride nodded.

"I'll phone Cecilia so you'll have a place to stay."

Bride nodded again. "Thanks. She won't mind?"

Her grandmother laughed. "Cecilia is up there rattling around in that big old house by herself since Bert died. She'll be glad you're there."

"And the money we talked about?"

"Don't worry. I got the money here in the house. Just worry about telling your mother."

As Bride slid off the couch, her grandmother spoke again in a quiet voice. "Is Wayne going?"

"To Toronto?"

Her grandmother smiled. "Where else would he be going?"

Bride shook her head. "No, it's just us. Me and Wanda."

∽∾∾

BRIDE SAT IN THE TRUCK waiting for him to come out of the store. Is there anything as sweet, as beautiful, as full of life, as giving in? It only tastes this good if you wait for it, she thought. When chocolate melts in your mouth, bitter, sweet and dark, the release is intense. I don't mean to resist, collapse, it just happens — chocolate icing, fudges, Black Forest cake. And Wayne. As delicious as any slow-melting chocolate.

I bet he doesn't see himself that way.

He came out now, smiling at her as he hurried toward the truck. He slid behind the wheel and put the truck into gear.

"You're beautiful," he said. "Right there, now, you're beautiful."

She smiled and thought, don't lie to me. And then she thought, sometimes you can lie by saying nothing at all, lie with a look, a touch. Mom and Wanda are lying. Not out-and-out telling me lies, but they are thinking things they won't say. I can see something going on in Mom that's got her all jumbled-up inside. Half the people in the cove know, or can guess, what's going on. I'm not sure I really believe that. I'm not sure what the lie is.

Wanda's another pack of lies, mostly in what she's not saying about Vincent. She's so desperate to get away. Not that she hasn't always wanted to get away from her life, but in the last few weeks she can't seem to talk about nothing else.

He spoke again, disrupting the flow of her thoughts. "Beautiful."

I'm not lying to anyone by not saying nothing, except maybe to Wayne. But this doesn't seem like a lie, because I think he already knows that I'm not going to be staying.

It's not a lie if you don't say the truth, but everyone knows what's really going on.

∽◦∽

JANICE STOOD BEHIND THE COUNTER, stacking packages of Player's Lights into the narrow shelves on the wall above the cash register. She did not hear Katie come in.

"Hey."

The sound of her voice stopped the motion of Janice's hands. She stood still.

"Hey," she said again, "can we talk?"

Janice turned. Katie stood with one hand on the counter. "I said I was sorry."

"I heard you. Why didn't you come up last night to study?"

Janice didn't speak.

"You were afraid."

"Look, I said I was sorry. Why can't you just leave me alone now?"

Katie put both hands on the counter, leaning toward her.

"So that's it, is it? You think you can kiss me and walk away because you're afraid? Well, I don't want you to do that."

She picked up a handful of black liquorice bits from a jar on the counter.

"You come and see me tonight." She held up the fist full of candy. "I'll pay you for these then."

∽o∾

"MOM." BRIDE SAID IT LIKE a fact, not a question.

Her mother went on removing the cans from the cardboard box, hand over hand, as if she were pulling in a net. From the time she was a child, her mother's hands had always been full — laundry baskets, brooms, bags of groceries. How could you catch a butterfly if your hands were always full of junk? Janice looked up, raised her eyebrows as if to ask the question, what do you want? but could not be bothered to vocalize it. After all, I'm only her daughter, and daughters are commonplace things that you don't even see right there in front of you. Unless they are out of place, like a pair of boots kicked off in the wrong spot or a dirty plate on the kitchen table.

"Well?" Janice had not stopped the unpacking, turning away to throw the box into the corner.

"So, how's it going?"

"What? I'm busy, how do you think it's going? Why don't you pick that broom up now that you're here and sweep down the aisles?"

Janice opened another box, not bothering to stop for Bride's reply. Bride walked toward the broom.

They worked in silence, the sound of busy hands, unspoken thoughts, filling the space between them.

"Bride, I see you with Wayne all the time now. I told you I don't think much of him. He's only using you, you know that, right?"

Bride stopped thinking about the speech she had been working through in her mind. "Is that your motherly advice? Don't trust Wayne?"

"Do you think he loves you?"

"I don't think nothing that I want to be telling you."

Janice frowned. "He wants to have a young girl around him, someone who'll look up to him because he's older. He needs to be with people who make him feel better about himself as a layabout, a hangashore, that's why he's hanging out with the crowd your age. And he wants a beautiful girl, too. You hear what I'm saying?"

Bride put the broom aside. "And what does Rupert want from you Mom? I guess you knows all about being used."

She walked out of the store, the door slamming behind her. Maybe I just don't tell her, she thought.

◦◦◦

JANICE KNOCKED. KATIE SAID, "COME in," from somewhere inside the house. She kicked off her shoes in the porch. A big grey cat sat on the edge of the mat in the entranceway. A large, rumbling purr came up out of his broad chest. "Montgomery," said Janice, bending over to rub her knuckles on the top of his head. "Big Montgomery. Where is she?"

"In here," said a voice from the living room.

Katie was sitting on the sofa, her arms folded, a book spread across her lap. She took her glasses off as Janice settled herself on the other end of the couch.

"So?" she said.

Janice hesitated. "You told me to come, so I'm here. I said I'm sorry already."

"You have nothing to be sorry for. Have you ever done that before?"

"Kissed a girl?"

"Yes, kissed a girl."

Janice looked down at her fingers. Her nails were chipped, and a hangnail on her pinkie made a red tear in the flesh. "No."

"Well, there's a first time for everything, Jan. The first time I did it, it scared me silly."

"You kissed a woman before?"

"Lots," said Katie. "But I don't think any of them were as lovely as you." She reached over and stroked Janice's arm. "You know those liquorice that I owe you for? Well, I don't think I'm going to be able to pay you after all. I think you will have to take them back."

She reached into a dish that sat on a table by the sofa. She picked one liquorice nib out and dropped it onto her pale pink tongue.

Katie pulled her tongue back into her mouth. "Come and get it," she said.

∽०∾

JANICE LAY IN BED. IT was warm in the nest of sheets and blankets, although the early July morning was still cool. The birds were up, flirting and fighting outside the window. The light had just begun to filter back into the world. The colour outside the window was grey, the air thick with an early-morning mist that might burn off if the sun came out strong. Rupert snored beside her.

She slipped her hand under the waist of her pyjama bottoms, her bare hipbone filling her cupped palm. Her fingers traced the bone, looking for a Braille imprint of lips. Perhaps the skin felt softer there now. She lifted her wrist to her mouth and inhaled. She could almost smell Katie's kisses, a faint hint of her saliva. She opened her pyjama top and squeezed her arms together, pushing her breasts up in the space between them. She could feel Katie's soft cheek against her chest, the silk of her hair tickling her rib cage. She ran her hand down her pyjama bottoms again. Still wet. The evidence is all here, she thought, her scent on my skin, the print of her teeth in my thigh. I feel like I have just robbed a bank. This must be what it feels like to sit in the back room of a bar with a shotgun on your knees, running your hands across a stack of crisp bills — illicit, powerful, glorious.

"I ..." Janice had tried to speak.

"Don't talk, now is not the time for talking." Katie held Janice's face in her hand as she kissed her, pushing her own candied tongue into Janice's mouth.

What am I doing? she thought as she kissed her. What in the name of Jesus am I doing? Blessed Saviour, don't let me fall. Janice could not stop her lips from reaching out for Katie again and again, drinking her in, a mouthful of liquorice. Janice shifted her lips to Katie's neck, sweeping the hair out of the way of her mouth. Katie pulled her head back to accept the kiss. Janice's tongue was on her collarbone, tracing the line of it, licking from shoulder to sternum, pushing the clothes away with her hands, following each rib to Katie's breasts with her tongue. Ribs. Protection for the heart. Katie's breasts were warm in her hands, the nipples pulled into cones. Katie inhaled deeply as Janice took each of them between thumb and forefingers, pulling gently. Bending her head down, she ran her tongue in the spaces between her fingers, slowly taking each nipple in her mouth. How, she thought, how do I know how to do this? Katie gripped her head, her hands over Janice's ears. All she could hear was the sound of her own blood, roaring like the sea in a conch shell.

Katie's head was thrown back so far that Janice could only see the underside of her chin when she looked up. With her hands still holding Katie's breasts, Janice traced the outline of the muscles on her stomach, sliding her tongue down until she touched the fabric of her jeans. As her hands slipped down to open the buttons, her mind flashed with the image of herself, as if she were watching the scene on video. She hesitated until she felt the pressure of Katie's hand on her head. Janice pulled the jeans down from her hips and hooked her fingers under the elastic of her underwear. As she pulled them down, the smell of Katie became heavy in the air around her. Just like me, Janice thought, but different. She closed her eyes and let her mouth find Katie, salty and hot, like seawater trapped and warmed in the shallow depression of a rock.

Now, she thought, now I have done it.

Lord Jesus, lover of my soul.

∽∘∾

WANDA WIPED HER NOSE WITH the back of her hand. Bride stood in the porch, struggling to make the screen door catch on its hook as the wind pulled it open. She slammed it and kicked her boots into the corner.

"So what's going on?"

"Nothing. Want a cup of tea?"

Bride shrugged and Wanda put on the kettle.

"Nan phoned Aunt Cecilia. She says we can stay there. You tell them yet?"

"Fuck, no." Wanda sniffed again.

"You sure you're okay?"

"Yep. So when are you coming up from down the sound?"

"We'll be back on Sunday evening for sure."

Wanda lifted the kettle off the stove. Her back was turned to Bride.

"When are you telling him?"

Bride exhaled.

"You're telling him, right?" Wanda handed her the teacup.

"Yeah, I gotta tell him. I can't not tell him."

"So?"

"So after the weekend."

Wanda sat at the kitchen table. She picked up the Carnation milk tin and began to pour it into her tea.

"I want to be gone by next weekend. I don't have much to pack."

"You telling them?" Bride jerked her head in the direction of the living room where Ivey sat.

"I'll tell the old man. She won't even notice." She put her cup back onto the table. "Fuck, that's awful. The milk must be off."

Bride shrugged. "Mine's okay."

Wanda stood and walked to the sink, pouring the hot tea down the drain. The steel sink made a popping sound as the hot water hit its surface.

"How much getting ready do you have to do?"

"Nan took the money out of the bank. I have to pack."

"Your mother knows, right?"

"Yeah. Well, no. I tried to talk to her the other day. I don't know what's going on with her. Maybe she won't care."

Wanda pulled at the strap of her bra, lifting it away from her chest.

"Maybe her mind is elsewhere."

Bride ran her finger around the edge of the cup. "You think it's true?"

"What the boys are saying?"

"Yeah."

"I don't know, they're all full of shit." Wanda fiddled with the strap again.

"Well, there's something going on with her." Bride took another mouthful of tea. "She's all happy one day, and the next she's going around with a face on her like ten miles of dirt road. Something wrong with your bra?"

"It's tight or something. This period is going to be a hell one. That's pretty weird though, for your mother I mean. She's always so," Wanda hesitated, "so miserable."

"I gotta go," Bride said, putting down her cup. "You sure you're okay?"

"Yeah, I just got this pain in my guts today. Everything tastes like horseshit."

∽∘∾

IN HER MIND, WANDA WAS packing, thinking how little she needed to take with her. She would use the old beige suitcase that Lynfield had dragged up the path last week, the one with the broken lock. She remembered the bungee cords under the front steps that she could use to hold it together.

Janice is going to shit. Shit a solid gold brick. Bride gone out of her reach. Wanda stopped cleaning the kitchen. What the fuck am I doing this for? They're going to have to clean up after themselves when I'm gone. She draped the dishcloth over the faucet and walked out onto the front porch.

Sitting on the top step, she could see the harbour. I won't have to look at this fucking hole no more. Water and trees. How did I get born in the middle of nowhere? The outskirts of nowhere actually — the suburbs of bum-fuck nowhere. How can you be anyone in a place like this? You need buildings and roads and shops and people. Some kind of framework for your life. Something to hold shit together. Otherwise, you just bleed into the water and trees.

I won't sell drugs when I get there, she thought, I'll get a real job. Maybe me and Bride can work together. In her mind, she could see them both, standing behind a counter, typing on a keyboard. She took out a cigarette, holding it between her lips as she searched for her lighter. The filter stuck to her dry lips, and when she licked it to loosen it, the roughness of the paper made her gag.

I hope this gut ache is gone by next week, she thought. I don't want to be sick when we leave.

✂

BRIDE STOOD AGAINST THE LIGHT of the window so that her face was frosted with shadows. She does look like me, Janice thought, especially now.

Bride started to talk, softly but quickly, not stopping for breaths between sentences.

"Mom, don't be mad. I would have told you sooner, but Wanda and me just decided, really. And don't be mad at Nan. She's just trying to help. And I'll have family to stay with. Aunt Cecilia is always good to me. She said it was okay for me and Wanda to stay as long as we liked."

"Aunt Cecilia? In Toronto?"

"Yeah. We're going." She swallowed. "To Toronto. Nan's giving me a thousand bucks."

Janice sat down quietly on the couch, looking out the window, past the place where Bride stood.

"You're not leaving." There was nothing of a question about the way she spoke.

"Yeah, I am."

"You're too young." Janice could only hear the sound of her own voice in her head. Bride's voice became softer, more distant.

"Mom, please don't make this hard."

"For how long?"

"I don't know."

"You're leaving me."

Bride's eyes were defensive, shifting as she tried to anticipate how her mother would stop her. "No, that's not it. I'm going to Toronto, not away from you."

Janice looked at her. "After everything I have done for you." She was shaking her head slowly.

"Please stop."

"You don't know what it was like being seventeen with a baby and no man. That's why I married Rupert — to give you a father. You think that was an easy thing to do? And now, you're going to walk away like it was nothing."

"Mom, it's not my fault what happened to Dad, it has nothing to do with this."

"Nothing to do with it? You had nothing to do with ruining my life? For me getting stuck here? You're free to leave with a good conscience then."

Bride turned toward the door.

"I wish you had never been born." Please don't let her hear that, Janice thought, it's a lie.

"What?" Bride stopped. She did not turn to face her mother.

"Home. I said, come home. You know you can always come home."

"Right," said Bride, turning in the doorway. Janice knew she had heard her right.

"I can borrow your blue suitcase," Bride said, as if she were entitled to it, as if she had won it fairly.

Janice nodded. Why did I say that, she thought. Why have I never told her that the morning she was born the sun came up as soon as she made her first cry, and that I looked in her eyes and saw her father, three months dead? Why have I never told her she is the reason I started to believe in God?

༄

THE NEXT MORNING, WANDA THREW up. She could hear the boys talking downstairs and the sound of furniture being dragged across the floor. Fucking little devil skins, she thought. As she sat up, her mouth filled with saliva and she ran down the hall to the toilet. The linoleum was cold on her knees. The faint odour of urine made her gag again. As she inhaled, her empty stomach lifted and she spat out a stream of saliva and stomach acid. It's a stomach flu, she thought as the liquid poured out of her mouth and nose. She said it out loud to make the reality of it more certain, more material.

"The flu."

I'm not pregnant. She did not say this into the empty room, but put her hand to her lower abdomen and pushed hard. I'm not. I'll be better before we go.

The knocking on the thin wood of the bathroom door made her lift her head.

"Fuck off."

"Wanda? Wanda, we don't have no milk." It was Corey's voice.

"I don't give two shits."

"Wanda, we don't have nothing for breakfast." He introduced a pleading tone into his conversation with the bathroom door. "Can you come down? You said not to turn on the stove ourselves."

"Fly to Jesus, will ya, I'm sick."

There was no sound from the other side of the door, as if Corey was trying to understand the relevance of her illness to his problem.

"So we'll wait for you to come down then? Can we use the toaster?"

She picked up the cracked-dry bar of soap from the edge of the turquoise bathtub and flung it at the door where the voice came through the wood.

"If I have to get up off this floor, I'll skin the two of you alive and stick you in the chip fryer."

She could hear the sound of small feet on the stairs, and then a voice said, "Is she coming?"

"Nah," said the faraway voice of Corey. "But we can use the chip fryer."

Wanda laid her face against the white plastic toilet seat and listened to hear if her tears made any sound as they fell into the water. The sounds from downstairs were small and purposeful now. Get up, she thought. She stood and opened the shear drapes of the window above the toilet, and she could see a motorboat heading out the arm. She's not going to tell him, she thought. She's not going to have the balls to tell him.

She turned the cold-water tap on in the wash basin and bent forward, twisting her hair into a roll and throwing it over her shoulder. The coldness made her feel focused and clear. She opened the door to the bathroom and yelled.

"You little fuck faces stay away from that chip fryer. I'm coming down."

She walked back to her room, thinking that a swollen belly would completely obscure her feet from her own view. She abandoned the thought before she would give herself permission to acknowledge it. And then she thought of Vincey. That prick. All smooth and sweet and big, manly laugh and trying to make me tell him what is none of his concern. I won't be telling him where I'm going.

She was dressing, and could see the outhouse from her window. For the first time, looking at it in the daylight, she realized that it tipped westward, away from the water, like a compass hand pointing her in the right direction. Bride better not let Wayne change her mind for her.

In the kitchen, she roared at the boys, who backed away from the kitchen table. She saw herself in the big cracked mirror that hung in the hallway — a skinny blond girl, waving her arms at two little boys who had emptied the cupboard of its contents. I have to go, she thought. Bride can't leave me here.

She thought about the two forms that she had seen in the boat, dark and tiny against the water. The white motorboat looked as small and fragile as an eggshell, broken open and emptied of its contents. She won't give in to him, Wanda thought again.

Maybe it's best she didn't tell him. I'll talk to her when she's back. Hopefully, she won't say nothing this weekend.

∽○∾

I MARRIED HIM TO GIVE her a father. No, that's not the whole truth, Janice thought. I married him because I was afraid to be alone.

But he isn't a bad father to her. She's almost his own. But him and Brendan were no more alike than chalk and cheese. Brendan had his own mother's sweetness, and her red hair. Brendan. She let herself imagine his face, and her hands could feel the silkiness of his hair when she touched him. For that moment she could smell his scent and, if she let herself go, she would be able to taste his skin.

Stop. He's dead. He's dead and gone. Rupert is my husband. Not the one I wanted, but the one I got. Sometimes you get less choice than you figure you deserve.

Now that she had started to think of him, she could not turn off her mind. Remembering had opened the box inside her, the place where she kept all the pieces of Brendan, and that night when it was over. "A wonderful-bad storm," Myra said. A storm that lasted for four days.

The winds that sunk the *Ranger* took no pity on the land that night. It piled the snow against the house to the eaves on the northwest corner. Janice and Myra sat by the woodstove after the electricity was lost. Come home, was all she thought. She sat and stroked her stomach, rubbing it like a magic lamp, wishing him back on the land.

"Don't you be worried," said Myra. "That little baby is going to be alright. Women are made to give way, bend and stretch and make room for others. You have room in you for her. You'll both be alright."

The phones had been down for the better part of two days, and most of the wood that Myra and Janice had been able to get into the house had been burned. The front door was snowed-in halfway up its length, so that if they opened it the drift would have collapsed into the hallway.

When Janice saw Rupert coming up the path toward the house the next day, he had a shovel across his back. The hooded parka hid his face, the moving snow obscuring the rest. She knew it was Rupert. Brendan would have told him to check on us, she thought. He was pulling his legs out of the thigh-high drifts, struggling against the wind. She waved from the window at the dim outline in the drifting snow, and he raised his hand back, but not in the usual way. The heavy lift of his arm made her think that something was wrong.

He shovelled himself into the house and stood, dripping onto the linoleum, the snow scree on his parka melting and sliding down the front of the nylon shell of his coat. His face was wet. Janice took it for snow.

"My love, he's lost," Rupert said.

"What?"

"Brendan is lost, Janice. The *Ranger* sank last night."

She felt Rupert put his arms around her, trying to prevent her from falling, buoying her up as the blackness flowed in around her.

∽०∾

VINCENT SAT IN THE BRANCHES of a tall spruce. He had broken away some of the smaller boughs, giving him a clear view of the backyard of the Stuckless house. The moon was behind a cloud and a summer fog had settled over the cove. This darkness might work in the cunt's favour, he thought.

He did not see her. He may have been sleeping when she came into the yard. He heard the sound of a door closing — a door snapping closed, like it was on a spring. It focused his senses. He was sure he could smell her, something musky, ripe, like the way the back of her neck smelled when it was slightly damp with sweat. He could hear thumping and the sound of metal, but could not see anything in the fog. He swung out of the tree, softly landing on the needles below.

Moving slowing through the trees, pushing bows out of his way, he prayed he did not step on a dead branch. If she caught him, she would kill him first and ask questions later. She was that kind of girl. He would have no chance to lie.

When he was at the edge of the yard, where the trees thinned and the fence pickets began, he heard the door again. She was walking away from the old outhouse.

Bingo, he thought, I've hit pay dirt. Tough luck for you, you skinny cow.

When he heard her footsteps on the front porch and the sound of her front door closing, he sprinted across the backyard like a soldier, head down, bent forward to the earth.

How hard can it be to find a stash in an outhouse, he thought, as he stepped inside. Hardly bigger than a breadbox. Vincent stood in the narrow toilet that still smelt vaguely of old shit and lye and turned on the flashlight. Spider webs hung in all the corners and a fine layer of dusty grime coated every surface. He looked around at the old tires, the plastic Rubbermaid tubs without lids, the broken hand-push lawn mower. Where? He held his breath and lifted the seat, the cuff of his jacket between his fingers and the cracked plastic seat. Nothing. Nothing on the rafters that held up the peaked roof.

Then he saw the toolbox, its tin surface shiny, free of dust. She had stacked the money together in piles, fives and tens mostly. The bills were worn. Not like a briefcase full of crisp cash, but it would get him the fuck out of this hole.

Oh Wanda. You were good for something after all. He took the small bundles of bills and tucked them behind the lining of his leather jacket through a tear in the pocket.

As Vincent walked down the hill toward the beach, the money shifted toward the back of his coat. Wayne's burgundy pickup sat parked next to the wharf. The water was almost calm, crawling up the beach in small waves. Vincent walked out onto the wharf and turned to survey the beach. No movement.

Excellent, he thought. Now we'll see about them keys.

The truck door was unlocked. He sniffed when he opened the door. The truck smelled of stale smoke and a girl-smell — perfume or shampoo.

No keys in the ignition. He slid his hand under the driver's seat. It was embarrassing to have to steal from people that made it so easy. He thought proudly of Wanda for a moment, sliding into the truck and closing the door gently behind him. The engine struggled to start for a moment, and then caught quietly. He drove up the road from the harbour slowly. The light had started to turn the clouds pink behind him, but the road was still dark, so he switched the lights into low beam as he drove up the hill. He stopped at the top and ran into the woods, picking up the bags with his gear that he had hidden in the alder bushes.

It would be a beautiful day, he thought, as he climbed back into the driver's seat. A beautiful day to get the fuck out of here.

∽⌒∾

THE NIGHT WAS DARK WHEN Wanda walked up the pathway to the house. No moon, no stars. A layer of dense cloud lay over the arm of the bay, making the night warmer than it otherwise would have been. She looked around as she stood on the porch, and when she was sure that no one was watching, she dropped into the long grass and ran to the outhouse. She held the door in her hand to let whatever light the night offered into the tiny black space. Wanda opened the toolbox. She dropped a handful of worn bills into the tin. Something's wrong, she thought. She knew this as she dropped the lid. She could feel that the box was too spacious, her fingers brushing against nothing as she dropped in the new contribution. In the dark, she opened the lid again and reached her hand down into the space.

The bile rose up in her throat as her fingertips stroked smooth tin. She opened the door and jumped down from the high floor of the toilet. The ragweed and grass that grew high around the toilet were heavy with rain and seedpods.

She was sick again.

∽◦∾

THE NEXT TIME WAS MORE intense. No words, no candy. Their hands shifted over each other, clothes opening, tangling their limbs. The progress up the stairs was halted with kisses and caresses, each step territory gained or lost by the touch of a hand, the wetness of an open mouth.

They lay in bed after, Janice holding Katie, whose head rested on her chest. Katie reached over and held her hand, stroking the knuckle of Janice's index finger with her thumb.

"What happens now?"

Katie snuggled in closer. "It's just like any other relationship, Jan."

"Do you want a relationship?"

"We've already got one."

Janice closed her eyes. A relationship. I've already got one. With Brendan. And Rupert. With men. Some of them still alive.

"If you were ..." Her voice stopped, but her thoughts ran forward into the unspeakable — I'd leave here with you and never look back.

"If I were a man? What?"

"Well, I'd know what to do next." Janice was looking at the ceiling.

"What would you do? You'd tell people right? People would find out. That's what happens when you care about someone."

Janice continued to stare at the ceiling.

"Your family will find out, Jan. Everyone is going to find out. We are not going to be able to hide this. How will you tell Rupert?"

"I didn't plan to."

Katie lay still.

"Oh, I see," she said. Her voice was small and bitter. "So, you think he's not going to find out? Do you think half the people here don't suspect it already? Before it even crossed our minds maybe?"

"I don't want everyone to know."

Katie released Janice's hand and pulled back from her.

"You should have thought about that before you kissed me." Katie rolled away, closer to the edge of the bed.

"Katie, I'm sorry. But this is really personal. I don't want everyone talking about it."

Katie turned to face her. "More personal than Rupert? You don't seem to mind that people know you're sleeping with him."

Janice did not speak. She thought, I don't sleep with him, just beside him.

"I didn't think you were a coward, Janice Marsh." She had gotten out of bed now and was walking toward the bathroom.

From the bedroom, Janice could see that Katie stood in front of the sink, brushing her hair, pretending not to listen to the sounds of Janice moving, waiting to hear her walk toward her. She turned the water on in the bathtub. The mass of her blond hair fell over one shoulder, the small sharp bone of her scapula made her look delicate, almost breakable.

Shit, shit, shit, Janice thought, hitting her fist into the pillow. She pulled her shirt over her head and walked down the stairs.

∽∘∾

IT HAD BEEN TWO DAYS since Janice had seen her. Those nights played over and over in her head. She would be packing groceries at work when the images would flash across the screen in her mind. Katie's small hand on her breast, her fingers cupped around it, her own arm draped across Katie's back as they lay in her bed. Every time she thought about what she had done, the sexual rush spread up from her lower belly.

How could she be so mean? Janice stepped over the mud holes in the path shaded by the stunted spruce. The earth floor of the trail was still moist here despite the July heat. The path was quiet now. When Janice was a child, it vibrated all day long as children ran along it, towels over their shoulders, to reach the pond. The spruce reached out their thin, green fingers, scratching at the small ribs of boys, their arms and torsos brown from the sun, the tiny pink trails in the flesh obscured by sunburn at the end of the day.

The sun had set and the last rays reached up from behind the hill, clinging onto the land. By the time she reached the edge of the pond it was dusk. No one sat on the big rock overlooking the water. It was a deep, brown pond, marshy and filled with water lilies at one end. The other end, the swimming hole, was clear of weeds and lilies since the depth there prevented their growth. A child could walk maybe ten or twenty steps out, the cold water rising up around their legs and torso, and then the bottom dropped, a sheer fifteen-foot fall.

Janice pulled her jacket tight around her as the wind blew across the water, cool now that the sun had set. It was almost dark when she left the pond, and by the time she reached the path, the sky was black. She skirted along the edges of it, her hands moving from tree to tree, her feet feeling cautiously for roots and rocks in the path. Then it ended, opening into a broader way that ran behind the potato fields, wide enough for cars, but grassy.

They must have been standing perfectly still, listening to her footsteps on the path, smelling her otherness on the wind, making a collective judgment about the threat she posed. When she stepped among them, she heard the shudder of a large body, followed by a quick snort. She could not even see their outlines in the blackness.

To her left she felt the tread of heavy hooves as the animal moved, perhaps toward her. She stepped to the right, away from the movement, and stretched out her hand in the dark. The warm bristle of horsehide seared her palm.

The horse, not even a shadow in this light, made a high-pitched and nasally snort at the suddenness of the touch. Janice felt the huge muscles of the neck as it flung its head toward her, breathing hot in her face as she pulled her hand back. The clattering of hooves shifting on the stones of the path jolted her, and she thought, they will trample me. All around her the large bodies moved in response to the one spooked animal.

Days before, she had seen the horses that people had released for summer foraging while the winter's hay grew on their own enclosed fields. Maybe twenty animals, mostly the small, tough Newfoundland ponies, sleek now that they had shed their long winter coats, but some bigger animals too, mostly grey and invisible in the fog and the dark. The animals walked slowly away from her. Seeing in the dark when Janice could discern nothing, they moved farther up the hillside to where the potato gardens lay.

The smell of the pond on the wind brought her out of the world of the horses. The brackish, muddy smell of the water mixed with the sweetness of the water lilies. The last remaining heat from the day clung to the evening wind, pulling together the scent of earth, water, drying hay and fresh white sheets snapping on a clothesline, as a woman stood on her toes to pull them down out of the wind's grasp.

She thought again of Katie. She doesn't know what it is like to live with judgment. If Katie thought that she'd be teaching school here if people knew, she had another thought to think.

All this trouble, this disruption and turmoil for a few frigging nights. She turned her collar up against the wind and walked out the mud path toward home.

∽०∼

JANICE STOOD IN THE PORCH, her head bent as she kicked off her shoes. When she looked up, her mother stood in front of her. Myra's face had the look of someone interrupted in the middle of a bad thought.

"Bride's took off for the weekend." Myra held the paper in her hand. Janice could see the big, loopy letters of her daughter's handwriting.

For the first time in days, she did not see Katie's face in her mind, obscuring her view of the world. Janice thought, I'm driving her away. She took the piece of paper from her mother's hand.

"Where? With who?" In her mind, she could see her and Wanda hitchhiking the TransCanada toward St. John's.

"I bet it's that Wayne," Myra said. "I'm phoning his father."

Janice stood holding the paper. "He's a grown man, Mom."

"He still lives in his father's house, so I'm phoning."

She heard the spin of the rotary dial and then her mother's voice in the hallway. Much of Myra's voice was muffled, but then she said clearly and more than a little anxiously, "Well, where did they go?"

Myra walked out of the hallway, her lips pursed together. "She's with Wayne," she said, not looking at her daughter. "They are down in Cooper's Cove. When Rupert gets here, don't tell him that she didn't tell us. We'll tell him we said that she could go. And don't tell him that they're are down there by themselves, either, say a whole bunch of them went."

Janice nodded. Yes, of course. They would make a lie. They would imply that they were still in charge of her.

"What else did George say?"

Myra was looking out the window now, glancing up and down the road. She spoke without turning her back.

"He said that they left early this morning. Packed up the motorboat and went." She pulled the curtains back to see better.

"They are gone until Sunday her note said. Did you hear any forecast?"

Myra shook her head.

So many secrets, thought Janice. So many truths that cannot be heard.

∽o∾

BRIDE SAT TOWARD THE BOW of the motorboat. The camping gear was stowed low in the bottom to protect it from the waves that splashed against the sides of the boat and sprayed the contents. Her head was tilted up, the wind whipping the ends of her ponytail around her face. She looked up into the cliffs rather than down into the water. The shape of her bottom on the seat made his mouth dry — compact, solid curves.

The shadow of an eagle flickered over the waves. The bird flew into the stunted trees that hung onto the cliffs. Wayne could see the dark shape of something made, not grown, sitting in a crook of roots far above the water. As his eyes picked out the nest, the big wings stretched out and she glided into it, sensing the danger in his line of sight.

It was wrong, he thought, to leave without telling Bride's mother that they were together. She had written a note and left it on the kitchen table. "Gone down the sound with the boys." He should not have told her that it would be okay. He looked at her again as she pulled the jacket closer around her to shut out the wind, her body shape outlined against the grey cliffs they passed.

Well, she wanted to go after all.

The entrance to the harbour was narrow and deep, a keyhole cut out of the rock. The faces of the tall cliffs on each side of the narrows stood impassive, blind guardians of an empty palace. The red, layered sedimentary rock was sheer from the tree growth at the peak to the point where it fell into the grey water. The channel was deep and clear of sunkers. Inside, the cliffs opened and the beach was wide, perfect for spreading and drying fish. It was a protected haven from the sea. The merchants had set up shop here and supplied all the little coves and harbours through the northeast arm of the bay.

That was then. Now there were only old houses that had been rebuilt and converted into cabins. Those houses that had not been renovated and propped up over the years had fallen, having slipped from their foundations after seasons of frost and wind, long after their builders had given up on this idea of home. A heap of broken roof slates were piled where the church had stood. Many of the grave markers in the cemetery had fallen backward into the long grass. Only stone endured here. The wood had all rotted back into the thin topsoil.

Wayne brought the boat toward the beach. The weekend cabin-goers had built a wharf. He came alongside it, holding the wharf railing with one hand, and jumped onto it to tie up the boat. They were the only people in the harbour.

Bride was unsteady as she stood in the boat, lifting her ass in the air while one hand held onto the gunwales. She stretched out toward the wharf, lunging toward it quickly when she realized she could not reach. Women's sense of gravity must be all messed up with all those curves, even the tall, lean ones like Bride, Wayne thought. The boat rocked and she clung to the ladder that was nailed to the wharf until the boat steadied, then climbed slowly up. From where Wayne stood, he could see the slight, muscular curve of her hips pull the wash-worn jeans tight as each leg advanced up the rungs of the ladder.

Merciful fuck, he thought.

As soon as she landed, Wayne jumped back into the boat and began to throw the gear onto the wharf, then he jumped back up onto the wharf, checking the knots in the ropes.

"Well, Bride, we better find a place to pitch this tent," he said, heaving it off the wharf.

He took her hand as if to lead her, but she stepped ahead of him and headed for the clump of trees on the hill above the ruins of the church.

"There's a pond in behind where this church was built. Let's set up in there."

❦

THEY FOUND A CLEARING ON the bank of Little Long Pond that was free of stones and roots and put the tent up. The wind ripped up the pond toward them, the black, murky skin of the water wrinkling under its touch. Wayne built a fire close to the shoreline — no beach here, just a muddy track around the water.

"This will keep the flies away. I found some blasty boughs to make it smoke." He pointed to the pile of dry branches that he had stacked up, the needles reddish-brown.

"The flies will be out as soon as the sun is down. Time to make supper."

"Alright. I just need a sweatshirt."

Wayne wrapped the potatoes in tinfoil and set them at the edge of the fire, covering them in ash and coals.

"I was always the cook when we were out on the boat," he said, flipping the pork chops in the pan, smiling at her, looking for some sort of recognition or approval.

They ate with their plates on their knees, seated on rocks around the fire. The sun had gone down behind the hill, the sky above red and blistered with the burn of its passing.

"Red sky in the morning, sailor's warning. Red sky at night, sailor's delight," he said.

She lifted her eyes to the sky.

"You're not a sailor anymore," she said, smiling a jagged, lop-sided smile that pulled the left corner of her mouth higher than the right.

"Once a sailor, always a sailor."

Wayne brought out his guitar from the tent. The flies sang and danced in the air above their heads despite the smoke from the fire. Bride pulled up the hood of her sweatshirt and drew the strings tight.

Wayne strummed the guitar.

"What do you wanna sing?"

"I'll just listen to you play."

He picked out chords as she stared into the fire, poking it occasionally with a stick. The moon had risen, but hung behind a mist that made it look sickly pale. The flies buzzed around them, biting when the smoke from the fire changed direction with the wind.

"These flies are driving me nuts," she said, jumping up. "I'm going in."

Bride walked toward the pond, pulling her shirt off over her head. When she reached the shoreline she stood only in her bra and jeans, her back to Wayne. He knew that she felt his eyes on her. In the firelight, the dip where her back narrowed before the flare of her hips was all in shadow, making her ass seem more prominent. She pulled off her pants and shoes and waded into the water. Wayne stood on the shore, the fire behind him, barely able to see the outline of her, limbs dark against the veiled moonlight.

"Bride, come in here out of it, you don't know this pond."

She continued, pulling her feet out of the muck with each step as she waded to the deeper water.

"Bride, there might be weeds, you could get tangled up ..." His voice trailed off as she bent to enter the water, the darker place where she stood dropping downward. The sound of the water as she entered it was soft and heavy, as if a smooth stone had broken the surface, clean and without a splash. He held his breath when he could hear nothing else, knowing she was under the water.

She came to the surface much further out in the pond with an urgency. She called to him when she caught her breath.

"Come in. It's not too cold and there are no nippers out here."

"Bride, get out of the water and I'll build up the fire," he replied, sounding almost stern, his own voice reminding him of his father's.

She dove again and he could hear nothing. Please Jesus, let her be alright.

She breached like a trout, closer to shore now, laughing. It was shallow and she stood to wade to shore, into the firelight. She pushed her hair back from her face. Her legs and arms were streaked with mud from the water. Her underwear and bra dripped rivulets of water down her stomach and legs.

"Here," he said handing her a blanket. "You'll get cold."

Bride stepped closer to the fire. Using the blanket as a tent, she crouched and flung out her bra and underwear. She looked at him, and he could see something in her eyes, something that was always there, but now seemed clearer. A mischief. A challenge. Aggression. Under the blanket she was naked, and he could see her thinking, knowing that he was imagining her bare skin.

Wayne stood back from the fire. She looked older in this light. No, not exactly older, but perhaps more sure of herself. Her eyes had almost no colour in the firelight. They were all pupil. All predator.

"Why didn't you come in?"

"Can't swim."

She shrugged. "Do you have anything to smoke?"

He nodded and walked back toward the tent, still thinking of her bare skin under the blanket. The sound of the zipper closing ripped a hole in the silence around them.

They smoked the joint in silence, listening to the sounds in the woods.

"Wanda's good weed," he said, exhaling. "For special occasions, she said."

"How come?" said Bride.

"How come this is a special occasion?"

Bride shook her head, her lips open, letting out the smoke. "No, how come you never learned to swim?"

"Not a good idea."

She giggled. "Why," she laughed again imitating him, "was it 'not a good idea?'"

"It just means that you freeze to death instead of drowning when you go in. It makes it longer. Half of the boys on the boat, when we use to go out, didn't know how to swim."

She was silent for a while. "I wonder if my father lived long enough to freeze. I don't know if he could swim."

Wayne lit a smoke. "You didn't know him, did you?"

"Nope. He drowned before I was born." She shuddered and pulled the blanket closer.

Neither of them spoke. The fire began to die down, burning into embers.

"You know about her and Katie right?" She turned her head to look at him. Her eyelids were lower now, half closed.

"It's true? I heard some boys saying stuff, but you know they're full of shit."

"I think it's true. She's in love with someone and Katie is the only one she spends any time with."

Wayne sighed and looked down at the fire.

"If this is a problem for you, I understand if you don't want to be with me no more."

"Why would I not want to be with you?" He was looking straight at her now.

"Well, I guess you'd be worried about me going dyke on you."

He put his head down and laughed. His shoulders shook. She was so earnest, so much openness in her face, so much courage. That is her weakness, he thought. She is brave and she will risk everything to prove that. He went over to the rock where she sat and draped himself over her, wrapping his arms close around her, his chin on her shoulder.

"Bride Marsh, you're right about me being in a state about you, but it has nothing to do with your mother." He held her tighter and kissed her behind her ear.

"You're mucky," he said into her ear. "Now I've got pond mud in my mouth."

She shifted her head to the side so that she could look at him. "You could have other tastes in your mouth."

"Such as?" He smiled.

"This," she said, kissing him.

∽o∾

WANDA STOOD IN FRONT OF the takeout, her hands in her pockets. She could not concentrate on picking the money out of the crowd of people that stood around. On a normal night, on any night except this one, she would have made a mental estimate of the night's take based on the number of people, the proximity of the day to the regular distribution of government cheques, the pay days of her regulars, and whether or not it was a holiday. People always buy more weed on holidays.

Tonight she could think of nothing except how she planned to haul Vincey's balls off. It would be a public castration. She would confront him out in the open, in full view of the boys whose opinions he found valuable. If he did not tell her where he had put the cash, she would hurt him. The blade of the knife was hot in the spot where her fingers held it, caressing the sharp edge. She knew exactly how she would do it. At the point where he raised his arms up, doing that she's-a-crazy-bitch shrug that all men did when they were cornered, she would pull the knife straight across his belly, just under the rib cage. A surface wound only, but he would bleed like a butchered moose.

I will make him cry like a little girl, she thought. Her mind focused on his stomach again, and how lovely it was at the point where the muscles layered under his diaphragm.

She took a deep breath inward. Can't get soft, she thought. He expects me to be soft, to be malleable. I need that money. That money is my life, and he's not getting my life.

Colin came around the corner of the takeout. He smiled at Wanda.

"Got any weed that's going bad that you got to get rid of? Anything that you think might be a bit poisonous that you got to give away?"

Colin was always broke, but he never asked her for a freebie without a joke. He knew that she was not a pushover. He never asked like she owed him anything, like he was entitled to anything. He offered to make her laugh in return for a bit of a draw now and then.

"You little prick," she said smiling.

Colin walked closer. "Willing to take any risk to participate in your drug trials, Wanda. I'll sign a waiver."

"Nothing tonight. You see Vincey anywhere?"

Colin stopped smiling. "I went down there this morning," he said, the fun gone out of his voice. "I lent him my knapsack last week, and I was going in the woods this morning." He paused. "He's gone, Wanda. I guess he didn't tell you, either. His grandmother said that he cleaned out his closet, but he never said nothing to her."

"What do you mean he's gone?"

Colin looked sorry for her. He made his voice gentler. He spoke to her like the left-behind girlfriend.

"He took off. His clothes and stuff is all gone. He fucked off. I think he owed some of the boys some money, too. Me, he just took my knapsack."

He just walked off with my whole life, thought Wanda. He just walked off with all my plans in his ass pocket.

∽◦∾

BEFORE HE OPENED HIS EYES, he heard the fly buzzing somewhere close to the nylon skin of the tent. The sound pulled him from sleep. At the same time, the curve of her body against his back made him hard. He could feel the shape of her breasts pressing into him as she breathed, her chest falling and expanding slowly as she slept. Her arm curled around him, her palm open, warm and relaxed against his skin. The soft length of her legs tangled with his own. He wanted to turn over, watch her face for clues as she slept, but he could not break the connection of his body next to hers.

The sun patterned the tent walls with branches. The nylon flexed in the wind and the poles that held the tent in place trembled. He rolled from his side to his back and she followed, pulling her hand across his chest as she moved. In her sleep, when he could not see the want in her eyes, she looked innocent. Black hair spilled against the sleeping bag. Her eyelids fluttered. The skin below her eyes was transparent, with a bluish tint that would become more pronounced as she aged. Her forehead was smooth and untroubled. Her lips were parted in sleep, as if to tell a secret that she could not say when awake.

She bit his lower lip between her teeth last night, sucking it softly in her mouth. When he placed his hands on her ribs below her breasts, she giggled and pulled deftly out of his grasp. It made him aware of the strength of her — the solid, wide rib cage that held up her breasts, the hard muscles in her abdomen.

"Don't. It tickles," she said, still a little stoned.

He held her arms at her sides and moved over her as if to pin her. Her biceps flexed and she jerked out of his grasp, sliding out from underneath him. He fell onto his stomach on the air mattress, not quite prepared for the suddenness of her movements. She slid on top of him, lying on his back, heavier than he expected she would be.

"Don't struggle," she said, her lips almost touching his ear, "you're not going anywhere, buddy."

"Yes, ma'am." He let all the tension leave his muscles. She grabbed his wrists, her arms on top of his, mirroring the bend at his elbows. She rested her mouth against his ear again, her breath warm on the side of his face. She took his earlobe between her teeth and growled, and gently moved her mouth down his cheek, running her tongue along the stubble at the hinge of his jaw.

"Turn over," she said, loosening her grip on his wrists.

He obeyed, and she lifted her body to allow him to roll over, then returned her hands to his wrists, spreading his arms wide as if in crucifixion. Her legs were tucked up so that her knees rested against his hips. She pushed her full weight into him and kissed him hard on the mouth. He let her tongue push at his own, twisting them like snakes, a double helix. Her hands stroked his chest, reaching immediately for his nipples, stroking them until he sighed. She lifted her head from his lips and placed her tongue on his nipple. He reached for her ass and held the firm roundness of it until she began sliding her mouth down from his chest. For a moment, as he held the back of her head, he thought, I can't breathe, and all the air left his lungs as she took him in her mouth. He gasped to fill his lungs and came, curling his head forward and lifting his chest.

She rolled over next to him, lying on her back, after he had loosened his grip on her. His chest still rose and fell in short breaths. He rose on his elbow and reached his hand out for her breast. She held his wrist for a moment before pushing him away.

"Not now," she said, rolling onto her side.

He moved against her back and pulled her into him.

"You," he said with pleasure in his voice, "are some shocking girl."

She laughed into the crook of his arm that lay under her head. "Aren't you the lucky one then?"

"Yes," he said, squeezing her hard. "Yes, I believe you're right about that."

⌀

LEVI SAT WITH HIS HANDS in his lap, cleaning the fingernails of one hand with the nail of another, dropping the imagined dirt out the open window. "So what you're asking of me, Wanda, is this — that I should trust you enough to advance you the merchandise on credit?"

Wanda nodded. "You don't have no reason not to trust me."

"My dear, I have reason to trust you. Our arrangements have always been that you make your purchase and I ask you no questions. I presume that you smoke what I sell to you. I sell to you on the presumption that you're the end user, the consumer. Now you're coming to me and suggesting that the product I provide to you for your own use is actually being resold to others. I'm not comfortable with this news."

Wanda stared at him as he continued to pick at his nails. "You can't be serious. I've been dealing for you for a year. You know I don't smoke that myself."

He looked up at her and smiled a gentle, knowing smile. "That was the understanding we had. I had no reason to suspect that you were re-selling my product." He took a tissue from a packet and began wiping the crevices and dials on the radio. "You see my position here, no doubt. You're now telling me that you are yourself, trafficking. You see the difficulties of that, obviously. I'm now selling to a trafficker, not simply possessor. This creates legal consequences for me that I am unwilling to accept."

"Look, I don't understand this. You give me a bit of credit, and I pay you when I've sold it. With interest." She paused for a moment. "Please."

He turned to look at her. "This attitude is what has kept our people down for centuries, Wanda. We are wedded to the truck system of the merchant class. The merchant gives you enough grub to get you through the winter and summer, and you give him your fish in the fall. A cashless economy. How can an entrepreneurial class emerge from that? I will not be accused of perpetuating this repressive economic regime."

Wanda could feel the bile and rage mixing in her stomach. I'm gonna puke, she thought. If I puke in his truck, he will have a stroke.

"Levi," she said, changing her tack, "we've done business for a long time now. That first time, you gave me credit. I'm asking you to do that again, but we can change things a bit. I'm willing to make this worth your while. You increase the price, say, twenty percent more," she paused, "we can even expand the product line."

Levi stopped cleaning his nails. "My mind is made up, Wanda. I'm not a man that you can persuade, manipulate or bargain with. This is not a negotiation tactic. I am telling you, no."

She could see the revenge in his face. "Then you're telling me that you're shutting down my business."

"Wanda, you're being emotional. You're being dramatic. We are a people given to hyperbole, and ..."

Wanda opened the door and stepped out. "This is fuckery, you maggoty little cunt. Well, this will come back on you, my son. This is all about me not going along with your plans last month." She slammed the door hard.

"Wanda. This notion of karma is a very primitive one, and not one that I subscribe to," he called after her.

She turned to see him spraying the Windex on the seat and the door of the truck where her arm had been resting, knowing that she was watching. He bunched tissues together and wiped the vinyl down as she looked on, oblivious to the insult.

∽⚬∾

BRIDE REALIZED THAT THEY WERE in a graveyard when they found the old headstones lying under the long grass. The dense mat of vegetation was thick over the earth, obscuring everything. They set about discovering the stones. Wayne leaned forward, bending at the knees and resting his hands on his thighs, trying to read the grave markers.

Bride thought, I'm never going to see this place again. Maybe I will never see him again, either. How do you know if you love someone? I'm in love with his forearms and how powerful they are against my own skinny arms, the salty sweetness of his flesh, the way he stands, chest forward, eyes level, legs apart, the way he laughs when he really laughs and can't hold back, when the masculine deepness gives way to a giggle.

I wonder if Mom is thinking this, too. Maybe if you loved someone before, you can be sure when it happens again. I guess she loved my father. She never said. If you were in love before, is the next time something totally new, or are you just trying to replace what you lost? Maybe it wouldn't be as easy to love someone when you're old and you have all that history. Her love was making her sad. I don't want this to end with Wayne and me being sad.

I love the touch of his hands on my skin and the way that being with him makes me feel. Bride looked over at him, squatting now in front of an upright stone. It was going to be hard to leave him.

She walked over to him, laying her hand on his shoulder. Some of the headstones lay flat, covered in the grass. They could have read those that had fallen backward if the words had not been covered with moss or lichen. Bride knelt in front of a stone, pulling the grass back from its face.

"In Loving Memory of Cecil Jacob Hart. Born December 3, 1889. Lost at Sea September 1922. Loving husband of Dinah." Bride read out loud. "In my Father's house are many mansions ... I go to prepare a place for you." The last line had been encrusted with lichen that filled in the form of the letters. She read it haltingly.

She looked down at Wayne. "I think we might be related to them," she said, rubbing her thumbnail across the words, "Lost at Sea." Then her hands found another stone in the grass. "Dinah Maria Hart, 1890–1923." She looked down at Wayne again. "She died right after him. Jesus God."

Then with Wayne's help, she found the little stones, white with carved lambs on the tops. George Elijah, age eight. William Henry, age six months. Bride sat on her haunches and stared at them, running her hands over the rough stones.

"Can you imagine it? Your husband drowns, your boys die and then you die yourself. I wonder if she left any other children."

Wayne stood up. "It was hard times back then, Bride. There's a lot of sorry stories in this ground."

Together they pushed back all the grass and picked at the lichen with their fingernails. Many of the stones had smashed in the fall and lay in pieces in the grass, some now embedded in the earth. The names were all familiar to this bay. The Taverners. The Coopers. The Harts. The Whalens. Some had died out or moved on.

He took her hand and led her out of the graveyard. The evidence of their search looked wrong — the stones uncovered like the war wounds of old men, scars best left unseen. They sat on the hilltop nearby and laid back in the grass, watching the wind herd the clouds westward across the sky. The easterly wind was warm now, but in it was a hint of the cold that would come when the sun went down.

"What do you think their story was?" she asked, not taking her eyes off the clouds. "Do you think Dinah went down to see him off before he got aboard the schooner?"

"To go to the Labrador?"

"Yeah," she said, closing her eyes so that she could imagine the scene more clearly. "He went to the Labrador for the summer. Maybe she could stand on her porch and see him roll the molasses keg up the plank. Do you think she kissed him goodbye? Or do you think that she was so busy with the youngsters ..." She paused. "She was too busy, and then maybe she regretted that." Her eyes opened and she looked straight at Wayne. "Oh my Lord Jesus. I bet she was pregnant with William Henry when he drowned."

"You're one for making up stories Bride," he said, pulling her in tight so that her head rested on his arm.

"I love stories. Tell me your stories."

"Sure I don't have any stories. Anyway, you knows about all there is to know about me." The sly humour in his voice made her raise her head. He smiled.

"Oh, you big arsehole," she said, digging her fingers into his ribs. "I mean your stories, your family stories. You can't have a story on your own."

"My family. Oh, Bride, I don't know. We've always been here. We came from England, I suppose."

"No, not where you came from. Your stories. You know, the ones your father tells when he's half cut."

"The stories that my father tells is not fit for your ears. Girls getting knocked up on longliners, that sort of thing."

She pressed her fingertips into his ribs again. "No, not that. You know, old stories."

"True stories?"

"No. They don't always have to be true to be important."

Wayne shifted so that Bride's head lay on his arm and he could look into her eyes.

"Well, there is one story that George tells, but it don't make any sense. He tells this story about being down on the Labrador when he was just a boy, really. Aboard his father's schooner. They'd anchored outside this cove because the rocks were supposed to be treacherous in it and no one knew where they were. George's grandfather was an old hand and he always gone north on the schooner. He knew every crook and cranny of that coast, every rock and every shoal. But the old man was dead by that summer, and no one knew how to get into the cove, so they anchored outside it, but not too far outside, because the water was deep when you got off shore a bit."

"So George was asleep this night, when he heard this woman singing. He couldn't pick out none of the words. He pulled on his boots and went up on deck. When he did, he saw that they had lost the anchor and were drifting into the cove. He called up all hands and they got out of there."

"Did anyone else hear the singing?"

"Nah, they all made fun of him. So the next day, he took the dory and went in the cove hisself, but there was no house or nothing in there."

"That's weird. Like a reverse siren."

"Like a what?"

"A reverse siren. Sirens were these women that lured sailors onto the rocks."

"You paid more attention in school than I ever did." He sniffed, as if smelling the air, and exhaled. "No sirens in Newfoundland, easy enough to end up on the rocks of your own doing. Besides, I think women ghosts are good luck."

"You think women are good luck?"

"Not good luck, but good warning maybe. Women, dogs and horses. You all seem to have this nose for trouble. You know when there's a storm coming. Women are always getting men out of trouble."

"You think so? Why?"

"Well, women have this much more practical approach to danger. It's not like men don't know when something is dangerous, they just seem to think that they are more capable, stronger than they really are. I seen it on the boat all the time, men thinking they could keep their balance on the gunwales with a big sea on, and then over they'd go, ass over kettle, and we'd all have to scravel to haul them out."

"But some women are too afraid," Bride said. "Mom's afraid for me to pick up a knife because I might accidentally disembowel myself. She sees danger where there's none. Like in you."

"Well, your mother's a special case, Bride. But she had some hard knocks. Your father gone, just like that," he snapped his fingers, "and maybe she's right." He smiled. "Maybe I am dangerous."

Bride ignored his comment. "I know she had it rough, but she's fucking hard to live with sometimes."

"Well, we're all hard to live with, Bride. That's the point."

"Are you saying that you think that I would be hard to live with?" She raised her head up off his chest.

"I think that the only way that I could live with you is if you were on the flat of your back."

She was pinning his arms again now, and he was laughing. The wind blew her black hair into her mouth. She tried to spit it out rather than move her hands. He laughed harder. The water of the cove below was turning grey as the blue left the sky. The laughter and the voices echoed across the water, falling flat against the hills on the other side of the harbour.

～○～

WANDA WAS CLEANING THE UPSTAIRS of the house. Cleaning always made her mind clearer, more focused. She ran through the scenarios in her mind. No option to sell more weed. No other way to make money. Steal it, perhaps. She thought, who will have enough money to make stealing worthwhile? She stopped herself from thinking more on this, not liking the outcome.

She leaned over to run the mop under Ivey's bed. There were wet streaks through the dust and cat fur. She bent to reach into the corners, resting her hand on the bed.

It was wet. She raised herself up and touched it again. She pulled back the blankets and leaned over to smell it. Piss. A pool of piss seeping into the mattress, too much to come out of a cat.

She picked up the bucket and went downstairs to the kitchen. Ivey sat with her hands in her lap, staring out the window.

"Are you getting dirty now?"

Ivey turned her head. "Time for my pill?"

"I said, are you pissing the bed now? Is this your new way to get attention?"

Ivey smiled. Wanda put the bucket down on the floor and put her hands on her mother's shoulders.

"You better not start this, you hear me. I spends enough time cleaning up after you. But I'm not doing this, you understand?"

Ivey smiled again. Wanda's fingers dug into the fatty softness of Ivey's shoulders, shaking her, gently at first, looking into her eyes.

When Corey came into the kitchen, Ivey's head bounced off the back of the rocking chair as Wanda flung her backward like a fat rag doll.

"Wanda," said Corey. "Wanda, stop that, stop shaking Ivey." Then he looked around the kitchen, seeing the cold stove and the lack of dinner preparation.

"There any dinner?"

Ivey started to cry. Wanda pushed past Corey, grabbing her coat from a hook before slamming the door.

೧∞೧

THE WIND DID NOT DIE down. By morning it was strong enough to pull the nylon out of their hands as they struggled to take down the tent. Although the spot they had chosen was sheltered by a thick stand of spruce, the tent crinkled like wax paper as the wind blasted in off the water and over the hills of the cove, increasing its strength with every blow. It fed off the energy of the things it enveloped. It took strength from the salt water, fine particles of sedimentary rock, spruce needles and the fur of rabbits. All this stolen loot gave a physical presence to its otherwise formless self.

They were both awake by dawn, the time when the woods should have been grey and silent. The wind had blown stronger and stronger throughout the night and by dawn the cables that held the tent to the frame were coming loose. Bride lay listening for a long time, thinking about the wind. Her arm was around Wayne's waist, her face against his back. When he turned over, she opened her eyes and said, "We had better get this thing down."

He nodded and pulled himself out of the sleeping bag, searching for clothes in the half-light. She looked at the length of his back, the long muscles that flexed under his freckled shoulders as he stretched his arm out. Long arms, not skinny, but not bulky. He half stood in the tent to pull his jeans on.

"You'd better get up, Bride, we're going to have to break camp now."

He started to pull the clothes around the tent floor into bags and unzipped the door, stepping outside. She dressed quickly and rolled up the bedding. She pulled her hair into the collar of her jacket and followed him. The wind made it difficult to rise from the crouching position in which she had emerged from the tent. He was packing up the cooler. When he saw her, he said, "Come help me while I take this down."

She held onto the nylon as he took down the poles. Folding the tent was impossible in the wind, so they stowed it into Wayne's knapsack. The trek out to the harbour was as quick as they could make it. Once out of the protected grove of spruce and fir the wind was bitter cold, even for here. The knuckles of Bride's hands were red, and when she touched her neck, the coldness of her own fingertips made her flinch.

They set it all down on the wharf, then Wayne hopped down into the rocking boat. The force of the waves pushed them into the wharf. He loaded as quickly as he could, then pulled Bride from the ladder as she climbed down and placed her close to him in the back of the boat.

"Wear this," he said and she struggled into the life vest. He pulled one over his jacket and threw off the rope that held them to the wharf and they started out of the cove.

Coming out through the narrow opening in the rock, she saw the work that the wind had made of the water. As far as she could see up the arm of the bay, there were small, white caps of foam where the waves rose and broke in rapid order. They were not the long, rolling waves of a steady wind on an open sea, but rather choppy, tight, little waves, the result of a wind that blew in blasts. The stern of the boat sank as it rose over each wave, the nose tipped high in the air, blocking their view of the water. Bride sat clinging onto the seat.

"Get down lower in the boat," he shouted. "Kneel."

She spread her knees wide as she knelt, trying to avoid the salt water that had gathered in the middle of the boat. She turned to look at him. He did not meet her eyes, but was scanning the water, his jaw tight. The wind pushed back the fine, brown hair that usually hung over his eyes, and she could see that he would be balding some day, like his father, and that perhaps it would make him an even more handsome man. It would show the strength of his jaw more clearly. The fine blue of his eyes would be more pronounced.

I'm putting my life in his hands now, she thought. I won't do this again. I like my life in my own grasp.

∞◦∞

HE WAS STRATEGIZING, PLANNING TO take them as close to the shore as possible and off the open water of the arm, but not so close as to be pushed up on the rocks. He looked for a path through the gauntlet of waves. Rough water made him think of his father. The stories that George told of being out in rough seas were a part of his thoughts as he looked for the way. The time that he almost foundered the longliner on rocks in a big sea off Bluff Head. Taking the horse across the sound in a squall, George's own father trying to calm the animal as George sculled the punt, the horse kicking out the seats of the boat. Wayne thought, this is not skill. You don't stay alive on the water because of skill or learning. This is about luck and nerve and instinct. It is about not being foolish enough to think that you are the enemy that the sea has chosen. You are just a little speck on it, in the way of her fight with the wind. None of this is about you. You are just in the wrong place, at the wrong time.

He looked at the water around The Motion and knew that this attempt to get home was a mistake. The Motion was a shelf of rock, like a slice of sedimentary pie that sat off the very tip of the island. It was slanted, tipping toward the big island on a forty-five degree angle. On the high end sat an unmanned lighthouse. Before Confederation, a family lived there on a tiny piece of barren rock looking toward County Cork or Devon or wherever home had been.

The depth of the bay varied, with huge round pockets sunk into the bottom where the remaining cod stock over-wintered in the deeper, frigid water. He saw them every time they passed under the longliner, the screen of the fish finder suddenly falling off into an aquatic black hole. The depth in these places registered up to 450 feet.

The Motion rose up from a shallow shelf of rock that stuck out into the much deeper waters of the bay. The times that he had come around it had been relatively calm, and the bottom came up to meet them, like some huge mammal rising up from the deep. Forty metres at best.

The waves that were divided by The Motion were long-rolling and heavy, built on the open expanse of the Atlantic. When they hit the shoals on the shelf, they stacked up onto each other, like a panicked crowd trying to flee a burning building, no space for their strength and speed to dissipate. The tides also flowed past here at a rapid pace, splitting at The Motion into two separate arms of the bay. Rough, rapid water being pushed up an incline made The

Motion treacherous. The water did not flow, but moved cross-purpose to itself, "all higgly-piggly like," as George would say. And on wild days, The Motion boiled.

He had made a mistake. The bottom of the boat was puddled with water now from the spray of the waves. Taking them around The Motion in this squall was not an option.

Bride's voice drifted past him on the wind and he looked down at where she sat, one eye still on the water. "Turn around," she screamed at him over the wind.

He did not respond with words. Nodding, he began the slow, careful turn that would bring them back to the harbour, this time with the wind to their backs. The water was coming over the stern now. Bride shifted her knees further apart as the water collected in the bottom. He touched the back of her coat and she turned her head.

"Move up a bit," he yelled over the wind.

She crept forward, sliding her body over the seat without standing.

"Get that tub," he shouted.

She reached for it and began bailing, most of the water becoming airborne as she lifted the plastic salt beef tub over the side.

She bailed. He steered. When they rounded the last head coming into the cove, the water seemed calmer. When his hand touched the wood of the little wharf, he exhaled and, for the first time, realized that he had been holding his breath.

∽◦∾

THEY DID NOT UNLOAD THE boat, but took only their sleeping bags, mostly wet now from the spray. Taking her hand, he pulled her up the bank to where the renovated houses stood, cabins for the weekend visitors.

The door to the first house that they reached was not locked. Never lock a place of shelter in an unsettled place. The houses themselves were "owned" by squatters, who renovated the old abandoned houses into livable cabins. They came on the weekends in the summer.

The kitchen of the house was enormous, and a large day bed stood against one wall, the wood stove cold and black against the other. The pantry was a narrow galley off the kitchen. A large table dominated the rest of the room. Wayne set the sleeping bags down and Bride removed her wet jacket. The storm door banged in the wind as Wayne left again. He appeared moments later with an armload of wood.

"I think this is Neb Penney's cabin. We'll have to leave a few dollars for the wood and the use of the place when we leave."

In several more trips, he had filled the wood box that sat next to the stove. Through the old, three-paned windows, they could see the sky begin to darken, as black clouds rolled over the cove. The wind threw the rain against the glass, smacking the panes loudly with big, flat drops.

Bride sat on the day bed as he made the fire. Wayne put in the splits with curly, shaved edges that would burn quickly. A few pieces of paper and the flames started to flicker. He opened the vents wide, so that the flame could feed. Then he put the big chunks of birch and spruce into the round holes of the stovetop. The crack and pop of the dry wood were the only sounds in the room. The noise of the fire made her feel safe.

"You hungry?" he asked warmly, standing with his hands on his hips in front of the stove. "You must be. Let's see what Neb keeps in his pantry. I'm not going down to the boat in this rain."

They looked, pulling out tin canisters of flour, cans of beans and fruit, dried peas, potatoes and carrots and a bucket of salt meat — evidence of recent use of the kitchen.

"I sees a big pot of pea soup with dumplings in this cupboard," he said, kissing her quickly on the neck as she peered into the back reaches of a shelf.

He directed and she assisted, peeling the vegetables as he cut up the meat and put the pot on to boil. When he took down the bowl to make dumplings, shaking out the flour without a measuring cup, adding the baking powder with a flick of his wrist from the tin, she stood back to watch. He cooked with confidence, like a woman who had been feeding a family for years. She watched as he pulled together the dough for the dumplings with his hands, the flour catching in the hair of his wrist as he kneaded, the long, masculine muscles of his forearms flexing as he expertly dropped the dumplings into the pot of soup to cook. It made him more beautiful to know that the same strong hands that could pull up a boat for the winter could also mix dumplings. A man should not be afraid of gentleness, of delicate things, she thought. Real strength is knowing the appropriate force to apply to a task.

What he did out there today, she thought, I could not have done that. He has a skill that I don't have. For the first time in my life, I actually felt grateful that someone else was in charge. The boat seemed so thin between my knees and the water.

∽∞∾

IT WAS DRIVING RAIN THAT fell in sheets at an angle to the ground. Wanda stood looking at the back of Bride's house. The windows were all closed, but they would not be locked. Wanda knew the door would not be locked, either. She could see a light on in the living room and hear the low sound of television laughter. She walked through the woods behind the house until she could see the driveway. Empty. Roop would be up to the club. Janice would be up to Katie's. Wanda grimaced when she thought of them together. It seemed wrong. She felt sorry for Roop — he was the one that Katie was stealing from.

Not as wrong as this, she thought. What am I going to do if Myra wakes up? Am I going to hit her? How can I hit Bride's grandmother? And how am I going to get out of here? I don't know how to hot-wire a car.

The image of her hitting an old woman made her legs feel wobbly and the bile started to bubble in her stomach again. She sat down on a wet rock, pulling out her pipe, shading it with her hood as she lit it.

She saw herself sitting in the woods, ass wet, high, and thinking about hurting someone. Someone who didn't deserve it. Someone who wouldn't expect it. Someone good. Hurting Vincey would have given her a sense of pride. Myra would probably wake up and say, "Wanda my duckie, what is you doing?" She would be surprised and confused, not even afraid because they knew each other. Wanda was ashamed of herself, ashamed that she had even thought of this.

She got up and walked through the woods, back toward her house, slipping sometimes on the wet ground. In her stoned state, the smell of the wet woods overwhelmed her senses. It was like being stuck in a car with a pine air freshener, the windows rolled-up tight. This plan was the kind of thing that Vincey would think of. She stopped and bent over, vomiting on the side of the path.

I think I can do better than that, she thought.

※

THEY ATE LATE IN THE afternoon, the sky almost black with rain, as if it were twilight. Wayne found an old kerosene lamp and they tidied the kitchen in the shadows that it cast, flickering in the drafts that snuck in between the clapboard and the spaces along the windowsills. Wayne checked on the sleeping bags, which he had hung behind the stove to dry.

"Might as well pull out the day bed and set it up, we're not going nowhere this night." He did not meet her eyes as he spoke, but pulled open the bed and lay out the sleeping bags. Kicking off his shoes, he lay down on his side, his elbow supporting his upper body as he propped himself up.

"Come here," he said with a jerk of his head. He patted the space next to him.

Bride sat with her arms folded, leaning back in her chair. Her chin tipped toward her chest, her eyes looking up to see him.

"What for?"

"We got to keep warm. We're stranded, Bride. If I let you die of cold out here in the woods, your mother would kill me." A forced look of concern sat expectantly on his face.

"It's July, Wayne."

"Yes, but this is Newfoundland. It gets cold here in July. Especially at night." He patted the bed again with a serious, but encouraging look.

She stood slowly, unfolding her arms first, then placing her palms on the table and pushing back her chair. His eyes moved from her face to her breasts, which were squeezed between her arms.

"Perhaps you're a bit cold yourself?" she said with the same mock seriousness in her voice.

"Perished," he said, faking a shiver.

She walked slowly across the few feet of kitchen floor that separated them and laid her body down with the same languid motion, her hands on the sleeping bag, then one knee, then two and then onto her side. They lay facing each other.

"You will never believe how cold I am," he said. "I think I might be in danger of hypothermia. If you really want to save me, you better come right in close and share your body heat."

She wiggled closer, touching him, but there were still spaces of air between them.

"Well, that's better, but it's still touch and go. I might not make it."

She moved again.

"Better. Still a bit chilly, though."

She leaned in so that her nose was almost touching him, their bodies lay fully against each other now.

"Closer," he whispered.

"Jesus, Wayne."

They laughed, holding each other. He began to kiss the tip of her ear, her face hidden against his shoulder. He ran his tongue along the edge to the earlobe and began the slow descent down her neck to her collarbone. He slid his hand up and held her breast.

She pulled back then, just as she had done on the previous evening, moving his hands away and putting her mouth on his skin, as if to distract him from her own body. Last night he had let her trace out with her tongue the words that she would not say to him, but this time he pulled back from her kiss and her fingers opening the buttons of his shirt.

"Why can't I touch you?"

Her pupils, which had been large and open in the shadows that their heads made, now constricted as she drew back her head and the lamplight filled the space between them.

"I just don't want to, is all." Her voice was small.

His hand made circles on her back. "Bride, just let me see you, kiss you. I won't make you pregnant." As he spoke, he could see the questions and the mistrust come into her eyes.

"How do I know? How do I know that you won't do that?"

"Because I said so, Bride. You'll have to trust me."

She looked uncertain still. Then he saw the decision in her face. She sat up, removing her sweatshirt. She reached one hand back and her bra opened. She removed it, letting it drop to the floor. He reached both hands up and cupped her breasts taking her nipple into his mouth, pressing her backward.

She sighed and held the back of his head, her fingers tracing the nape of his neck.

"Please take those jeans off, Bride," he said, hoping, but not hoping.

She pushed him away and stood without meeting his eyes. She let her jeans and underwear drop to the floor. He held his breath, just as he had in the rough water. The perfect curve of her hips made his mouth water and he swallowed quickly. She lay down again, sliding her body against his.

"Let me kiss you down there," he said.

She did not protest, but the muscles of her thighs were tight under his hands. When she came, he could hear the surprise in her voice.

She lay next to him, in his arms, as he rubbed the top of her head with his chin.

"So, that wasn't so bad, was it?"

She shook her head, her bottom lip pouting. "I just want to

make sure that I don't get pregnant," she said, her face more serious again.

"I won't make you pregnant, Bride," he said, pulling her close. His face rested in her hair and he breathed her in. I won't make you pregnant now, he thought. Not yet.

❧

WANDA SAT AND WATCHED THE rain come down. The wind forced it to the west so that it fell on a slant. She got up to put a birch log against the woodhouse door that banged against the wall each time there was a gust.

Tobacco made her sick now. The only thing that settled her stomach was the special weed. She lit the glass pipe, holding her lighter above it, almost burning the top joint of her thumb as the flame curved upward.

She sat watching the rain, letting the smoke take the edge off the world. She could feel her digestive tract bubbling and gurgling. She could feel every air molecule that she pulled down into her lungs. Shit, a body stone, she thought. I will probably be able to feel this baby, too. Poor fucker. It's not the problem, really.

The baby can go away. That's manageable. But what the fuck am I going to do with no money? Without enough to make a deposit on a stash. She had counted the money again. One hundred and forty dollars.

She looked at the house from where she sat. No sound except the wind and rain moving through the trees and long grass. I never saw anything so lonely, she thought. How can that be my home?

❧

BRIDE WAS WATCHING HIS CLOSED eyes, looking at the tiny blue traces of veins in his eyelids. He seemed to know what to do out there today. I didn't. I just wanted to go back. I thought I was a coward first, and then I saw that he was afraid too. That's when I said to go back.

That didn't scare me as much as letting him do what he just did, though. Maybe I said yes because I was still upset about the boat. Maybe it was all just nerves.

She stroked his eyebrow with her little finger. His breathing was deep and even. Now is the wrong time, she thought. I'm not ready for him yet. I have to go.

THE NEXT MORNING THE SEA WAS dead calm. Rupert stood on the edge of the government wharf, surveying the results of yesterday's wind. The waves had forced the kelp high up onto the beach, where it lay tangled in black-green knots. By tomorrow, it would be brown and dry, the salty bladders deflated. Among the uprooted kelp were shimmering clear jellyfish, some of which were dark red and blue at the centre. Pieces of sea-battered wood lay grey and smooth among the white Javex bottles and the pink detached limbs of a doll. Blue and green shards of sea glass and jagged, smashed fragments of seashells flecked the beach.

There was no sign of them on the water. He had been up since dawn, sitting in the big chair by the window, thinking that perhaps they would come up at first light. He listened for a motorboat, but no sound echoed in the arm. He pulled hard on his cigarette, smoking it down to the butt in several powerful draws. He thought about Janice. He thought about how she always looked impatient or tired each time she turned her face to him. She had no more expectations for him.

I'll find Bride for her, he thought.

GEORGE WAS PUTTING THE KETTLE on when he saw Rupert walking down the lane toward the house. I might have known, he thought. He had been up since 4:30 himself, an old habit. Why is it when you're old and have nothing to do, you can't sleep, he thought. Last night he had slept poorly, even for him. The wind seemed to be constantly slamming against the house in powerful gusts. Every time he woke, he thought of Wayne. Thank Jesus he did not come up around The Motion yesterday. George had spent most of the day standing in the back bedroom of the house, looking down the cliff to the water. The waves washed up the beach to the base of the cliff, boiling and foaming amongst the rocks. George was a reader of waves. He could look into the water and see patterns the other men could not. It was not a matter of knowing where the rocks and shoals were. George would look out his window in the evening, surveying the cove. You see the way that lop comes in around Bluff Head, he would say to Wayne. Well, I don't like the look of it. I don't think that we will be going out tomorrow. A man who can read the water is a man who will stay alive. He thought, I hope to Jesus that he took one look at them waves yesterday and battened down for the night.

The front door slammed and George turned to see Rupert standing in the kitchen in sock feet, his boots left on the porch.

"Drop a tea, my son?" George held the kettle he had just removed from the stovetop.

Rupert's face was tight and hard. When he raised his hand to wipe the back of his mouth, George noticed that the fingers of his left hand were stained yellow with nicotine. Rupert shook his head at the offer of tea and sat at the kitchen table. The smell of salt herring hung in the kitchen. A loaf of fresh bread lay on the counter, a slice removed.

"Missed breakfast. I can put on a bit more herring for you."

Rupert shook his head again and met George's eyes for the first time.

"You don't have a beer, do you?"

George noticed for the first time that his hand shook a little.

"Not at five o'clock in the morning, I don't. A bit early."

Rupert laughed, but didn't smile. "Or a bit late at night. Did he tell you?"

"Who?"

"Wayne. Did he say where they were going?"

"Left a note that he was going down to Cooper's Cove, that's all. And that he would have the motorboat for a few days. I didn't know he took Bride till Myra called."

Rupert breathed out quickly through his nose. He searched around nervously in his coat pocket for a cigarette. Then, remembering he was inside, pulled his hands back out.

"Think they will be up soon?"

George laughed. "They are young people. They don't get up in the middle of the night like old men. I would say they'll be up by dinnertime. It looks like it'll be a fine day, no wind, so Wayne will come up today. He knows I wants the boat soon."

Rupert's face did not relax. "I don't know that Janice wants Bride to spend so much time with your boy. She is awful upset about this. Not herself, not herself one bit."

"Is that what you come here for? To give me messages from your wife? I guess she still thinks you're good enough for that — to be her messenger."

Rupert's hand was shaking again. "What are you getting on with?"

"Nothing. I just think if Janice got something to say to me, she should come and say it to my face, not send you as her messenger boy."

Rupert pushed his chair back from the table. "What did you mean by, 'she still thinks I'm good enough for that?' What do that mean?"

"Nothing."

"Tell me what you're talking about."

The poor bastard don't know, George thought. "I never meant nothing by it. Nothing."

Rupert got up and turned toward the door. "Just tell me if you hears anything from them. Like I said, she's right upset."

The door slammed. Poor fucker, thought George, looking at the clock and then glancing out the window to the cove.

∾o∾

MYRA AND JANICE SAT AT the kitchen table. Janice still wore her housecoat and her hair was stringy. She held a cup of tea in both hands. There was a bloody trail near her right thumbnail where she had torn away a hangnail. Cold toast, soggy with butter, lay untouched on her plate. Myra stood motionless, staring out of the window above the sink. Neither woman moved at the sound of boots on the porch or looked at him as Rupert entered the kitchen.

"Well, George don't know when they'll be up. I told him to call us as soon as he had word of them."

She looked quickly at Myra, grabbing the cup.

"Mom, read the cup, tell me where she is."

"You want me to?"

"Yes."

"But I thought that was a sin."

Janice folded her arms and looked away. "I'm willing to take that chance."

Myra dragged her chair from the table, standing on it to reach the tin where she hid the loose tea underneath the cinnamon, mixed peel and vanilla.

"My God, Rupert, help her," said Janice.

He went over to hold the chair, and Myra handed down the tin to him first and then took his outstretched hand as she carefully stepped down. They sat in silence as they waited for the kettle to boil again.

She turned her back to them and poured the boiling water over the leaves. Janice was crying when Myra turned around. Inaudibly, a stream of tears was rolling down her cheeks.

"Oh my trout, she's okay. I can feel it in my bones. I don't even have to read the leaves." She put her hand on her daughter's shoulder.

Janice sniffed. "Read them anyway, Mom. Please. I just would feel better if you read the leaves."

"Well, swirl the cup then. She is your girl. She is closest to you. You swirl it and tip it over."

Janice flipped over the cup, letting the liquid pull the leaves down the sides of it. Myra lifted it gently and set it back down in the saucer. Janice came around the table and stood behind her mother.

"You'll have to step back, I can't see anything with you this close."

Janice stepped back, her arms folded across her housecoat. Myra stared at the cup in silence. The tea leaves were spread all over the cup, none touching. It was a bad cup. But not bad for Bride or Janice. It was a bad cup for someone. She pushed it away.

"Well, what is it?"

"She's alright, she's fine. She'll be home soon."

"What's wrong? You look like something is wrong. You aren't telling me what you saw, are you?"

Myra turned to her and Janice could see the worry in her mother's eyes.

"Tell me, Mom."

"Bride's alright, I promise. I just saw something else there that I don't like the look of. I don't know what it is, Janice, but I don't think it has anything to do with Bride."

⌒⚬⌒

JANICE HAD NOT INTENDED TO ask her to come.

Rupert had come home at dinnertime. No sign of them, he said. Then Myra asked if George would take them in the longliner. She had, for the first time in days, stopped thinking of her beautiful face, the face that made her ache and long and ache again. But when Myra said to get dressed, to get ready, that they were going to look for them, she put her shoes on and walked up the hill. One foot after the other, every step a dread and a hope. Please let her not be angry, she thought. Please. I just have to tell her this.

The warm breeze lifted the curtains in Katie's windows. The drying clothes rose and fell on the line. The screen door was closed.

Through it she could see the soft outline of her sitting in the kitchen. When she put her hand on the door, Katie turned, and she could see the anticipation of something unpleasant on her face. Not anger, not fear, but a resignation that something conflicted and unpleasant would happen — as if it were all pre-arranged, fated. Janice could see that Katie was expecting something less than tragedy — anger, hurtfulness and sorrow, but not this thing that she brought to her now. She went in thinking, I don't know if I have the concentration to do this, to sway this course that her mind has already taken.

"Bride is lost," she said and stepped toward her, taking Katie in her arms. "She didn't come home."

Katie pushed herself back to look into Janice's face. "Lost?"

"She went down the sound with Wayne and they didn't come up after yesterday. I'm so frightened." She collapsed her taller, larger body into the other woman's arms.

"Come with me. We are going to look for them. And I need you. I need you to come with me."

Katie touched the tears on Janice's cheek. "My love. I'll get my coat."

∽◦∾

IT WAS NOT A LONG boat ride. Rupert stood on deck smoking cigarettes, lighting each with a short, deep inhale that pulled his cheeks inward. He scanned the shoreline and watched Janice as she stood with Myra and Katie on deck, their backs to him. George was steering, taking them on a steady steam down the arm, the shale cliffs with their stunted trees standing like a citadel on either side of the water. Viewed on an angle in the sunlight, the top layer of seawater looked almost emerald, but straight down was impenetrable blackness. Depth is like height, Rupert thought. That's what makes people afraid of the water. They are afraid of heights. He looked over and wondered how far below the bottom lay. It would be like falling off a cliff, except slower. He pulled back from the railing and looked again at his wife. Her back was rod straight and her shoulders were pulled up toward her ears. Her posture made him think how easy she was to break, like glass. No give.

I don't want to have to see her break, he thought. Please, dear Jesus, I have never done nothing for you, but if you care about her, listen to her prayers.

❧

KATIE STOOD AS CLOSE TO Janice as she could without touching. Her long blond curls blew in the wind and caressed Janice's bare collarbone, exposed by the same breeze. Does she love me, she wondered, and then guilt filled her up. I should not think of such things now, not when she is so full of worry. I'm a selfish woman. She looked at Janice's face. A line ran from her nose to her chin, the place where her cheeks lifted when she smiled. I want, she thought, to kiss that line away, to make her smile, to make her laugh.

How greedy I am, she thought.

❧

THEY WERE JUST OUTSIDE OF Cooper's Cove. George saw it first, bobbing in the water, the square corners of the cooler impeding its progress through the waves, giving it a stilted and bouncy jaunt. The cooler's white cover shone against the blackness of the water. He cut the engine and walked up onto the deck, the hard sound of the rubber boots hitting the boards. The women looked up and Myra said his name, but he did not answer her. Rupert stood with a lit cigarette in his hand, not smoking. George reached the cooler with a long-handled dip net. He coaxed it close to the side of the longliner, and with the net and some poles, he pulled it on board, the old cooler that he and Wayne took to put beer in when they had tourists out on the boat.

He set it on the deck and pried the lid off. The others stood around him. Inside was a half loaf of homemade bread, a jar of pickles and assorted biscuits that Bride had taken from her grand-mother's cupboard. He heard Janice start to cry, with big gasps of air between the exhaled sobs.

"The tent," said Rupert. The purple and grey nylon floated off the starboard bow, close to the shore. No one looked up.

"George," he said, as the tent passed them by, slightly under the surface, webbing and billowing like a giant jellyfish. George turned and looked at it, making no attempt to retrieve it. Overhead, the gulls spun and weaved and cried out with throaty voices, their oval orange eyes on the cooler, waiting for the people to step back from it.

∽○∽

JANICE HAD SUNK TO HER knees slowly, the strength leaving her legs. Katie's hand rested on her back. The only sound that she could hear was the sound of her own voice, silently asking for reprieve and denying the truth. Please, please, please. No. Somewhere outside her she could feel the others, but she was alone. She heard her own voice rise, and the sound of pain poured out of her, unable to stop. It felt as if it were something alive and as separate from her as a child being born, struggling out and making its own life. She folded over, her body in Katie's lap and her cheek on the deck of the boat. She was no more aware of the scent of long dead fish in the boards than she was of the colour of the sky or the sounds that Katie made to comfort her. Her body felt as large as all the world, as if there were nothing more to the universe than her immense and painful self. She was all the pain and sorrow of the world.

Myra looked over the side at the tent. "They are not drowned," she said. "I knows they are not drowned."

George and Katie turned to hear her, wanting to believe her words. Janice lay still, no words or touch could reach her. Rupert sat on a bench, quietly looking down at the wet cooler that spread rivulets of salt water across the deck, reaching out toward where his wife lay, her body in Katie's lap.

∽∘∾

BRIDE AND WAYNE WOKE LATE. The sun was a perfect ball of yellow that hung in the centre of the sky. All the rain from the night before had evaporated, leaving the grass cool at the roots. Bride's head rested on Wayne's chest, her ear above his heart. She breathed in his smell — popcorn and apples. She settled her head closer. He sighed, and she felt him breathe that first quick, deep breath of a conscious being.

He stretched one arm above his head, squeezing Bride into him with the other, mashing her cheek into the wide bones of his chest. She slid one leg over him and her foot rested between his feet.

"Morning, my angel."

She tilted her head and smiled up at him, eyes full of warm blue sleep.

"What time is it?"

"Late," he said, making no attempt to rise. "We'd better pack up and get home, they'll be worried."

"Yep. They will." She cuddled closer. "Worry that is."

∽∘∾

THEY SLEPT AGAIN AND THE sun rose higher. When the sweat that their bodies made woke him again, he could not say how much later it was. He rubbed her lower back, just where it curved in away from the hips, but before it opened into the broadness of her rib cage. The skin there was as soft as a fish belly, but warm and dry. Jesus, he thought, dear, dying Jesus. I touch her and my fingers ache for more of her. If I could absorb her through my fingertips, I might do something valuable with these hands.

She reached out her tongue, licking circles around the nipple closest to her mouth and his bones melted.

"Wayne?"

Her voice focused his mind, but his body was elsewhere.

"Um."

"Can you do that thing again?"

"What thing?"

"You know." Her voice was shy, and without seeing her face he knew that she was smiling, just a little.

"Oh, that. Well, perhaps I could, if you really want me to."

"Yes." She paused. "I really want you to. Please."

∽o∾

GEORGE KNEW HIS SON WOULD not have taken them out on the water yesterday. He was not a fool. Not a boy for book learning perhaps, but no fool. And he believed Myra when she said that they were not dead. Myra believed because she knew it, not because she could not imagine and understand the possibility of horrible loss. She did not speak with the wilful blindness of someone looking at a plane crash and hoping for survivors. She knew it like she knew the smell of her daughter's hair, or how much flour was in her pantry. So George believed her. It was like the way he knew the water. Myra seemed to smell the air for them, listening for a sound that no one else would hear. Dogs, horses and women. They know. They always know. He believed her, even if he could not smell the scent of them with his own nose.

∽o∾

WAYNE LIFTED HIMSELF TO A sitting position. Bride lay on her back, one arm on her chest, which rose and fell quickly. The look of complete release on her face — the eyes tightly closed, the mouth open — made him proud.

The longliner steamed into his peripheral vision. The movement outside the window drew his attention and his eyes flicked away from her and then back. He was smiling at the power he had over her, to make her cry out like that, when his mind considered what his eyes had seen. The longliner. In the harbour. Now. He reached for his jeans. Bride sat up.

"Get down, my father's out there."

"Your father?" Bride was lying on her back again, the sleeping bag pulled up to her chin. "Why?"

"Fucked if I know. Looking for us. Get dressed — for the love of Jesus put your clothes on."

He was gone before she found her underwear, jogging down the hill to the wharf, elbows pointing off to the sides, bare-chested in jeans and running shoes. The longliner steamed toward the wharf.

ᴄᴏᴏ

"WAYNE," MYRA SHOUTED. "GEORGE, IT'S Wayne. Take us ashore."

Her mother's voice pulled Janice from the place that she had gone. It took a moment for her to come back into the world with the rest of them, not quite believing that Bride might be saved. Katie was struggling, trying to push her away and raise her to her feet at the same time. Her lips were moving but Janice could not make out the words. It was as if the whole of the world were under water, swaying with unseen currents, distorted by the density of the liquid.

She was on her feet, Katie behind her, someone shouting, and then she saw him. A ghost. A drowned man running down the hill, pale even in the brightness of the sun. I'm seeing them dead now. I thought that they would live forever in my mind, but I can see them dead and walking. I want to remember them alive. I don't want to see this.

Janice was focused on Wayne running down the hill toward the wharf when her daughter appeared on the hilltop, black hair lifted by the warm wind of the day. She doesn't look dead, Janice thought. Her cheeks are almost pink. When she raised her arms in the air and shouted at them, her voice was as real as a seagull's cry. And then she knew she had been wrong, foolish, to give her up for dead. Her chest opened up and the lead weight that pulled her heart down like an anchor let go, and she was floating.

She turned to Katie, whose lips were parted as she smiled at Bride coming down the hill. Janice kissed her with the passion that had run in to fill the void left by the departing pain.

∽o∽

AS SOON AS GEORGE SAW him, the living, breathing, running form of him coming down the hill, he was angry. When Wayne stepped onto the wharf, bare-chested with the smell of that young girl all over him, George was mad.

"What have you done with me Jesus boat?"

Wayne looked perplexed, gazing down the length of the wharf as if he could not believe that the boat was not there.

"Boat was tied up here. I tied it up yesterday." He kept looking down at the water.

"Well, she's not here now, is she? That's a brand spanking new motorboat. Your gear is floating out the arm." He pointed over his shoulder with his thumb. "So I would guess that the boat is out there too, somewhere on the bottom."

Wayne paled. "But I tied it up here. Yesterday."

"Well, you must have been some cunt-struck when you tied it on because it's not here now." George pointed at Bride who had run onto the wharf, standing behind Wayne, shrinking back a little as he waved his finger at her.

Wayne continued to stare at the water. Bride took his hand, squeezing it tight and he turned to look at Janice and Katie.

∽o∽

THEY ALL WATCHED JANICE KISS Katie. That was the thing that did it, Bride thought, the anguish and grief and worry and pain. She thought we were lost, dead. It was like Mom couldn't keep up the lies and the unspoken truths and the fences that she had built up inside herself. Maybe tragedy brings out the worst in people. It seems to me that it just takes all the bullshit away. Tragedy brings out the truth in people.

〰〰

THERE IS A SOUND THAT water makes when it flows though the legs of a wharf, when it strokes the shore, that is almost welcoming. The interaction of the fluid and the solid is a wooing, a convincing, an enticement. Come, the water says. Come and be with us. Water is always a multiple, a collective.

Almost morning, Wanda thought. It will be light soon. How do you describe that point when the night gives up? It is dark still, and there is no line of light advancing, pushing back the dark sky. There is no clear break between the light and the dark. No shoreline. Water at least knows its boundary. It is aware of the place where it ends and the solid begins. Light permeates the world and draws out of it at will.

This first morning light would be grey. I'm going to die on a grey day, Wanda thought. She wondered now if someone were looking down on her, if they could see her standing alone in a boat, untying it, would they wonder what could be so wrong that this made sense? Would they look down and wonder how anyone could be that proud?

There was no one to see her. There was no one to wonder what an eighteen-year-old girl intended to do with a stolen dory. There were no other boats on the water. A woman with no money has no choices, she thought. She pushed off from the wharf. The oars were heavy and made for a man, for someone taller, with larger hands. It took her some time to understand that the weight of them was to her advantage in moving forward. She made slow progress toward the near point of land that marked the westernmost boundary of the cove. She needed to be around the head before the old men were up looking out of windows. The houses all clustered around the harbour.

She stopped before the point and let the water rock the boat. She kept the oars in the water and stirred them slowly to stop from drifting up onto the cliffs. Only the roofs of the houses were visible, no smoke from the chimneys. A light came on in Wayne's house. She rowed around the point and out of view.

She dropped one of the two anchors she had stolen over the side, the silver colour of it flickered in the black water for a moment, then was gone. The rope made a soft hiss against the wood as the anchor shot downward. She sat in the middle of the boat and picked up the second anchor. The metal was cold in her hands and for the first time she thought about how cold the water would be. She reached her hand over the side and slid the tips of her fingers in. It was instantly numbing. This will be quick, she thought. The rope that the second anchor was attached to was new, the yellow nylon itchy against her back, exposed where her shirt had bunched up as she wrapped it around her waist. She wound it like a bandage until it was thick and bulky. Then she knotted the rope of the anchor that sat in her lap. And then again. No way to untie that in the dark.

It was awkward to move like this, making it hard to pull up the other anchor that lay on the bottom. The boat would have to drift after she had done with it. The light had come into the sky now. She would have to work faster, before anyone sped by in a motorboat and wondered what a woman was doing anchored along shore. Double anchored. She looked across the water — forest, high cliff, the faraway lights of another small cove preparing to wake. No way was prepared for me, she thought. Nothing was done to make it easy for me.

"I tried my best."

Nothing around her was moved by her words. There was no response. Not even the eagle on the cliff face flew out of its nest to acknowledge that it took some solace in her words, that it too had felt a burden in being alone, unguided.

She was drifting out into the middle of the sound, into the deep water. She stood. The water was black. She lifted the anchor into her arms and fell forward, rolling into the water, the anchor clutched against her chest.

The shock of the cold was so intense that it opened her mouth, but the cry she made was dispersed through the whole of the ocean, blended with all the other sounds, so that there was almost nothing of Wanda in it. Her voice was now a part of something much bigger than her. The water was cold and it closed around her in a blanket of darkness. She had let go of the anchor, but it remained fastened tightly around her middle. She slowed for a moment as the anchor left her hands and the rope lengthened toward the bottom. The yellow nylon was long enough to give Wanda a moment of suspension. She hung there curled, a fetus in a chilled amniotic fluid. As the rope became fully extended, the anchor brought up on the end of the line. The taut rope bore the full weight of the anchor, and Wanda was jerked by her torso toward the bottom, arms and legs outstretched, a wild starfish. It was too dark to see the blondness of her hair at this depth.

∽∘∾

I HAD IT ALL FIGURED wrong, Bride would think so much later. Home is the place that you never leave.

When they got back to the cove, Wanda and Vincent had gone. And so had Wayne's truck.

"Them fuckers. I know she was your friend. Shit, she's my second cousin. But what kind of fuckers takes a man's vehicle? What kind?"

Colin tried to speak but Wayne interrupted.

"She never said nothing to you about this?"

Bride shook her head. She thought, she still is my friend. Why does stealing your truck end our friendship?

No one took anything that Colin said seriously because Colin never said anything serious. Except now.

"I don't think Wanda was in on it," he announced to Bride and Wayne. "I don't think she knowed. She had a face on her like a blood-poisoned cat the night I told her he was gone. I would say from the look on her she most likely went after him." He paused. "I hope for his sake he was driving fast."

"Wanda Stuckless was no innocent party," said Derek. "Wanda might not have left with him, but I can tell you, mark my words, that the two of them was partners. They were together all summer. Vincent was up to something with her."

"Had something up in her, more likely," said Leroy. The boys laughed and then became serious again.

"No, Vincent wasn't looking for tail. And Wanda was too smart to be tricked by that greasy maggot. They was a team."

Colin shook his head. "You never seen Wanda that night. You never seen the look on her face. It wasn't like she was just mad. I seen Wanda mad before, and this wasn't it. It was like someone kicked her in the guts. She went all slack when I told her he was gone."

"Well, if Vincent thought that he was going to get away on Wanda, he was a foolish asshole. That's the last thing you'd want chasing ya, Wanda, all full of the devil."

Why would Wanda chase him, thought Bride. Why do you all think Wanda was chasing anyone?

༺ঙ৹ঙ༻

VINCENT CAME HOME ON CRUTCHES a week after the dory washed up on shore, his head bandaged up. He was in a car accident somewhere in New Brunswick, his grandmother said. Late one night, some of the boys went over to talk to him after they were sure he was well enough to take a few blows. He never said anything about Wanda. No one could get him to say anything about Wanda.

Bride saw him sitting on his grandmother's porch smoking. As she walked up the path to the house, he looked at her and flicked his cigarette butt into the path in front of her. It was not aimed at her. He let it go with an easy, fluid motion that seemed relaxed, yet she could see that he was challenging her to come closer.

"So where is she?" Bride folded her arms across her chest.

He turned his head slowly. She could see that it pained him to do so.

"Who?"

"You slimy cocksucker, what did you do to her?"

He smiled. One of his teeth was missing now from the upper row on his left side. Bride wondered if it happened in the accident or when Wayne and the boys went to talk to him.

"What she wanted me to do." He thrust his pelvis backward and forward slightly, not breaking eye contact with Bride.

"That's not what I mean. I mean, where did you take her?"

"You knows Wanda, Bride. You think Wanda goes anywhere she don't want to? I left by myself."

"When I finds her, if you hurt her, I'll —"

He interrupted her. "You'll what? Hurt me? Well, I'm broken up already, what with the car accident and your boyfriend's bad temper and all. I'm the one that's hurt here, Bridie. Wanda fucked off and left us both now, didn't she?"

"You just mind yourself. You just mind, is all." Bride turned and walked away, knowing that she had been lied to. Knowing that he was false.

∽०∾

RUPERT STOOD IN THE PORCH, his boots on, his jacket bunched up in his hand.

"I just want you to answer me one thing."

Janice did not look up. She sat at the table, one hand folded over the other.

"Just tell me this. Was you always this way? With women, I mean?"

She looked up. "I don't know what you mean."

Rupert turned his head. "I mean, in the beginning, you seemed to like it with me."

"People change Rupert, and people get tired of being disappointed."

"Are you saying that I didn't make you happy?" He was unable to make eye contact with her.

Janice was staring at him now. "Rupert, I'm not blaming you for nothing."

"So are you saying that I didn't drive you to this?"

Janice sighed. "Rupert, this mostly don't have nothing to do with you."

"Are you still with her?"

"Katie?"

"Well who else do you think I mean? Is there more?" He looked at her now.

"No. There's no one else. I just want you to say her name."

"Are you still going with that teacher? Katie."

"No."

"So you gave her up?"

"I don't know."

"What do you mean, you don't know?"

"What's going to happen if I don't?"

Rupert slammed the side of his fist into the panel-boarded wall, which popped at his touch. Janice flinched.

"I'm going up to the club. Give me some money." He wasn't asking.

"I'll get my purse," she said.

∽o∽

"PLEASE," JANICE SAID. "PLEASE DON'T leave. Not now. I'm sorry."

"What are you sorry about?"

"For what I done." Janice looked out the window behind Bride's head.

"You talking about Katie?"

Janice's eyes were puddled with tears. "Yes. I was some foolish."

Bride put down the sweater she was folding. "Do you love her?"

Janice was wiping the underside of her eyes with the back of her hand. "No."

"You're a liar."

"Don't speak to your mother that way."

"I'm going to say what's true. You love her. For fuck's sake Mom, if you're not going to live with her, at least admit that you love her. You've never loved Roop. You can't hide that and you can't hide this. And I'm not going nowhere because of you."

"Then why? Because you're mad with Wanda?"

"No. Because I want to get away from here. I got no choices here, Mom. What am I going to do, marry Wayne?"

"You don't love him?"

Bride turned away. "If I'm telling the truth here, I would have to say no. No, I don't."

"You're not leaving because of what I done with Katie?"

She turned her head to look at her mother. "Not what you done with Katie, not because I don't love Wayne, not because Wanda fucked off and left me. Just because I need to. This is about me."

Yeah, Bride thought. This is about me getting frigging away from all of you.

∞

WAYNE TALKED ABOUT LEAVING, BUT Bride knew he wasn't going away again. He told her about living with friends, men who would always stay in small apartments with other men, using empty two-four cases as coffee tables. They would all talk about going home in the winter. After they had made enough money, they would get in their pickup trucks and drive east on the 401, while the sun set on the concrete they had poured and the pavement they had laid that summer. These were the same men who would give a girl in a bar a hundred dollar bill to buy cigarettes and tell her to keep the change because of the dimple in her left cheek, a dimple that reminded them of some other girl whose name was now forgotten.

Bride and Wayne sat on the wharf, looking out into the bay, out to the headlands where the water became serious. On a clear day you could see the Horse Chops from here, the massive rock that rose up at the head of the bay.

"I'm going to look for her."

Wayne flicked his cigarette butt over the wharf.

"Vincent's lying. He knows where she is."

"Well, he's not saying."

"We'll go make him say."

Bride laughed. "You tried that once. He would have said if he knew."

"Fucker won't even say what happened to my truck, and there is no way he don't know that. He just needs another punch in the face."

They sat in silence.

"Wayne, Wanda left when we were away."

"Left for where?"

"We were going to Toronto. I think she thought I wasn't going to go. So she packed it in."

Wayne shrugged. "She'll call."

"Well, she hasn't."

"She will." He smiled. "Why didn't she think you were going?"

Bride swung her foot against the timbers of the wharf. "You, I suppose."

He looked at her now, and she saw it again. That same sort of look, that what-I-want-from-you look. A look that said, "I got a plan about me and you."

"So ole Wanda is smarter than you thought. Had you figured. You'll catch up with her later. She'll come home."

Bride thought, you're not understanding any of this. He put his arm around her and pulled her into him, kissing the top of her head.

"Let's go back to the truck," he said. "The new truck. Thank the good Lord Jesus for insurance. It's getting cold out here now that the wind is up." He stood and pulled her up by the hand, and as they walked along the wharf and out the beach, Bride could feel a coldness that came from inside her, a chill not carried on the wind.

"Bride," he said, stroking her hair as they lay together in the truck, his arm holding her to his chest, the night air cold against her back. "It's time to give this up. Wanda's gone. We might never know what her and that fuckhead Vincey did, but I know she's gone. Without you. It's time for us to get on with it."

Us, she thought. Now he thinks he can make plans for me. Screw them and they think they can make up your mind for you.

"On with what?"

"On with our life."

So now my life is ours.

"Yeah," he said smiling and closing his eyes. "I got enough money to build a foundation, and I can cut the lumber. We could have a house by next fall if I worked hard."

"You really want that?" She lifted her head and propped it up with her hand. "You want me to stay here with you?"

He opened his eyes, and she could see that he was sensing for the first time that this was not what she saw as she fell asleep at night. She did not imagine them in a house up behind his father's place.

"I want us to have a home. To be home. Here. There's no need for you to go chasing Wanda."

"I'm not so sure that I want a home here."

"Well, this is where I'm staying."

"Perhaps we're going to be doing different things then."

He sat up, pushing her away from him. He expected that I would follow him, Bride thought. It has never occurred to him that I have my own plans and that I would make those without him.

"Wanda is fucked off without you. You might as well get used to the idea that you were left behind. And maybe that's where you belong."

∽o∼

THEY HAD TO PERFORM AN autopsy to be sure that it was her.

Wanda's body washed up on the beach two weeks after they found the boat drifting in the cove. The rope that she used to tie the anchor around her waist was still attached to the body, a long umbilical cord, leading back out to sea. The fingers were gone and there were no eyes, they said. I am glad that I wasn't there when they brought her up the beach, Bride thought. There are some things that you have to look on, even though you know they will follow you around and tear up your guts for years after.

People said that when they told Lynfield, he thanked the Lord that he was blind but wished that He had made him deaf too, so that he would never have to know what he had lost.

Wayne had come to see her as soon as he heard. They sat on the front porch. It had rained and the garden smelled like the shoreline of a pond. Water was dripping off the eavestroughs. Bride's face was wet. She stared straight ahead. Wayne's hand rested on her back.

"I know life is not fair," Bride said. "But just because it isn't, don't mean that I don't wish for it to be. I can get out. I could have just walked away and Wanda couldn't. She planned and saved and schemed and all I ever did was ask Nan for some money. She should have been the one who made it."

"You loved her," he said.

"Of course, I loved her. She was my best friend."

"Why am I not your best friend?"

Oh, for fuck's sake, all he can think of is himself. "Wayne, you want too many things from me for you to be my friend."

"What exactly are you talking about? You know, for a smart girl, sometimes you say stupid things."

"What I'm saying is true. You need me to be a girl, your girl, and you can't deal with the fact that I'm a lot more than that. You need me to be less than everything I am."

He bunched his fists up into balls on his knees. "I don't understand what you're saying. Why can't you just stay here and let me take care of you?"

"Because in the end, Wayne, everyone's got to take care of themselves. And I gotta go somewhere else to do that."

∽∘∽

ON THE DAY THAT WANDA Stuckless was buried, the sea was calm. Its mass undulated, rising and falling softly. The mourners sweated in their black suits and dresses, hot in the unexpected strength of the late summer sun. The wind was silent and still in the face of the congregation as they stood around the open ground.

Janice and Myra linked arms with Bride, who stood between them. They looked down at the box that was suspended above the grave. The officer held his book at chest height and read the last words. Bride could hear only fragments. "Our sister. Commend her into Your keeping ... it is not for us to question the Lord's judgment when he takes away one so young, as impossible as it is to understand."

That's all that you can really hope for, Bride thought. To get to a point where you accept what happens, even when it is so wrong. But to do that, you have to build boxes inside yourself, to contain it, to not let it mix with the rest of you, with the other boxed stuff. She looked at Katie, who stood with the other teachers, not acknowledging her mother. What would be the point of Katie standing next to Janice, holding her hand? They all know. Most people had stopped talking about it. What would be the point of confirming everything that they all know?

"Gone home to be with the Lord," the officer said.

Wanda's casket was lowered down to the bottom of the grave. Bride leaned into her mother as it began to sink. The officer threw the first fist of dirt, the hard clay pug that lay over the rock. The rattle of it on the lid of the coffin made Bride lean more on Janice and she felt her mother pull her closer. Wanda had come into the world alone and gone out of it alone. Home was the last place she would be going. Someone had driven Ivey and Lynfield and the boys here. They stood together, one of Lynfield's big hands on each of the boys' shoulders. Ivey stood away from them, looking over the heads of the mourners. The officer's wife, bony and frail, began to sing, her voice a surprise, a passionate plea from her thin, pale lips. Her voice rose, and the mourners stopped to listen, and then to sing themselves.

There's a land that is fairer than day,
And by faith we can see it afar,
For the Father waits over the way
To prepare us a dwelling place there.

In the sweet by and by,
We shall meet on that beautiful shore,
In the sweet by and by,
We shall meet on that beautiful shore.

Wayne took Bride's arm, leading her away from the grave. She thought, perhaps it will all resolve somewhere and all souls will be whole, and we will all be joined together. Perhaps there is a place where we can go, a place where the things that keep us apart will fall away, leaving just the gifts we can offer and the open spaces in us that we wait for others to fill up. A land where we will fit together instead of being torn apart. Or perhaps it will just end. No beautiful shore.

ACKNOWLEDGEMENTS

Thank you to Ian Cauthery, Aaron Schwartz and Lesley Buxton who, out of the goodness of their hearts, have read drafts of the manuscript in various stages of development and offered help.

In addition, a special thank you is owed to those who develop and teach the creative writing courses run by Ryerson University, the University of Toronto and the Banff Centre for providing a starting point for new fiction writers. The Wired Writing Studio at Banff deserves kudos for giving writers a place to write and a way to connect to others working in solitude across the country.

Thank you to Peter Taylor, my agent, for believing in the story. Thank you to Marc Côté and Blake Sproule at Cormorant Books for improving on that story.

Finally, thank you to Barry Stone for confirming for me, in a moment of doubt, that you do indeed scull a punt and row a dory.

Bev Stone